The Love Code

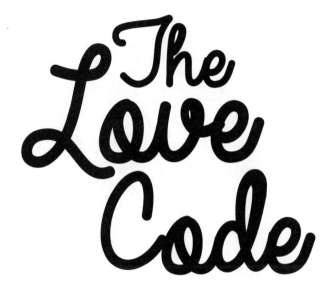

The Love Code

METTE BACH

JAMES LORIMER & COMPANY LTD., PUBLISHERS
TORONTO

James Lorimer & Company Ltd., Publishers acknowledges funding support from the Ontario Arts Council (OAC), an agency of the Government of Ontario. We acknowledge the support of the Canada Council for the Arts, which last year invested $153 million to bring the arts to Canadians throughout the country. This project has been made possible in part by the Government of Canada and with the support of Ontario Creates.

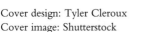

Cover design: Tyler Cleroux
Cover image: Shutterstock

9781459415867
eBook also available 9781459415850

Cataloguing data for the hardcover edition is available from Library and Archives Canada.

Library and Archives Canada Cataloguing in Publication (Paperback)

Title: The love code / Mette Bach.
Names: Bach, Mette, 1976- author.
Description: Series statement: Real love
Identifiers: Canadiana (print) 20200358235 | Canadiana (ebook) 20200358286 | ISBN 9781459415843 (softcover) | ISBN 9781459415850 (EPUB)
Classification: LCC PS8603.A298 L68 2021 | DDC C813/.6—dc23

Published by:
James Lorimer &
Company Ltd., Publishers
117 Peter Street, Suite 304
Toronto, ON, Canada
M5V 0M3
www.lorimer.ca

Distributed in Canada by:
Formac Lorimer Books
5502 Atlantic Street
Halifax, NS, Canada
B3H 1G4

Distributed in the US by:
Lerner Publisher Services
241 1st Ave. N.
Minneapolis, MN, USA
55401
www.lernerbooks.com

Printed and bound in Canada.
Manufactured by Friesens in Altona, MB in January 2021.
Job #271898

*The Love Code was written on the unceded territorial lands
of the Skwx̱wú7mesh (Squamish), Stó:lō and Səlílwəta?/
Selilwitulh (Tsleil-Waututh) and xʷməθkʷəy̓əm (Musqueam)
Nations where I am grateful to reside.
It is dedicated to front line workers.*

01 Life with Toppings

ASTRID COULD TELL from looking. She was just barely going to be able to reach the glass of water. The guy had placed it at the innermost edge of the table, farthest from where she was. She leaned across — stretching, stretching — to get the glass so she could move them along. When she was standing straight up again, they all laughed. Sure enough, her shirt was wet right where her boobs had landed in the puddle of water in the middle of the table.

When did my life get this crappy? she wondered.

Astrid didn't even recognize herself anymore. A year ago, Astrid would have been coming here with her friends. Coming in with her girlfriend Ivy. It would have been some other chump serving these guys.

Astrid's T-shirt with its happy frozen yogourt logo was soaked. Her face went red. The heat of humiliation stung her cheeks. She turned on her heel and walked away. She pretended it was the most natural thing in the world. Nothing was getting to her. Everything was fine.

Yeah, right, she thought. *What an utterly depressing job. How far can one person sink?*

She dropped the dirty dishes into the dish pit in the back. She went to get her bag, hoping that maybe, just maybe, she had an extra shirt in there. She didn't.

"And *that's* why you wear an apron," her boss said to her.

Everything is funny to him. Even my worst nightmare.

"Got it," she said. "Thanks." She snatched the apron he passed her and put it on over the wet patch down her front. She would have it for the next couple of hours. If she could crawl under a rock, she would. But instead she had to face the shop full of frozen yogourt fans. She tried to pull herself together by filling up the toppings. Nothing like moving mini marshmallows around with small tongs to make a person feel normal again.

"Let's go, Carson," said one of the guys. There was a smirk on his face.

Not for the first time, Astrid wondered if the guys made her life hard on purpose. The same group of guys came in every Sunday. And every time she ended up with a soaking wet shirt or feeling like she had just run a marathon.

Clearly, self-esteem was not a right in the world of yogourt retail.

02 Meet the Club

ASTRID GOT OFF the Commercial–Broadway 99 bus at the loop. Trying to make sense of the vast parking lot, she pulled out her phone to look for where she was supposed to be. It was cold and the wind made the rain whip against her face.

Slipping past grey towers, she finally found an old brick building. She felt like an imposter even opening the door. With each step she took, her stomach churned. She smoothed down her windswept hair.

Once she had her jacket off, she wiped the rain off her face with her sleeve. She took one deep breath and opened the door.

A small group of folks were all gathered at the far end of a room that looked like a workshop. It reminded her of Adam Savage's workspace, with tools and machines everywhere. There was a metallic scent in the air and it was colder than a classroom would be.

Everyone looked over at her standing at the open door. She proceeded toward them.

"And you are?" It was a tall Black woman wearing coveralls and a confident air.

"Astrid."

"Astrid. Welcome. I'm Aliyah. I run this thing. Sort of. I'm the official sponsor because I teach here at the University of British Columbia in Robotics. But this is a youth-led group, so I try my best just to offer guidelines and suggestions. And, of course, the workspace."

"Cool," Astrid said, "Sorry I'm late." The faces looked at her. She didn't know what to say back to them.

Aliyah pointed. "Bernie is the team captain. She was just explaining . . ."

Bernie wore flip flops in the middle of winter. She also wore sweatpants and a University of Waterloo scoop-necked shirt. "Eight weeks from now we will be unveiling our creation at the Robotics competition. It will go up against some fierce robots."

Astrid was impressed with Bernie's introduction and how she took charge of things. Bernie sounded like she knew what she was talking about.

"Ranj," Bernie said to the guy wearing a plaid shirt and thick-rimmed frames. "You know all about ballast, so we'll count on you for that."

Ranj nodded.

"And, Azi," Bernie went on to the other guy who was tall and thin. "You're our math guy."

"Yep," he said.

Astrid wondered who she was, what part she had to play in the group. What special skills did she have? Especially with math being taken, she didn't know what she could contribute.

The door opened again. In came a guy wearing full-on private school clothes. It was that Carson guy from the yogourt shop.

Aliyah said, "Late as usual, I see."

The guy set his briefcase on a chair and joined the group. Astrid waited for him to say he was sorry for being late, the way she had. She waited for him to introduce himself. He didn't do either.

"This is Carson," said Aliyah.

"With a K," said Ranj.

"And a y," added Azi. Azi and Ranj seemed to have a thing, like they both found the same stuff amusing.

"Oh, no," said Astrid. Then she covered her mouth. She didn't mean to say the words out loud. But there they were. *Not Carson*, she thought. *Karsyn*.

One name had terrorized her thoughts for the past year. Karsyn. Finally being able to put a face to it, the image made perfect sense. Of course he went to private school. Of course he harassed workers at yogourt shops.

This was the guy who had stolen Astrid's girlfriend, Ivy, from her.

Everything in her told Astrid to turn around and walk away. No way could she be in a club with this guy. Why was she here anyway?

"As I was saying," Bernie said loudly. She was clearly trying to stop any drama before it started. "We're taking a risk with the materials in the arms. But I think it'll pay off in performance. The thing is, we have to be really precise."

"That's true in all the sciences," Karsyn said.

Astrid rolled her eyes. She didn't know either of them, but she was annoyed that Karsyn interrupted Bernie. She didn't like that Bernie had to raise her voice to be heard over him.

Karsyn noticed the eye roll and shot Astrid a look.

Everyone in the club watched her and Karsyn. They felt the tension between them. They were waiting to see if things would escalate.

Astrid shook her head gently. This was not the time or the place. She tried to concentrate on what the team captain was trying to say. But she couldn't help but fixate on how cruel fate was. There were many reasons her life had fallen apart the April before. And she and Ivy were having their issues. But when this guy came along and swept Ivy off her feet, it was a real blow to Astrid. Before she could figure out what was happening in her own life, Ivy was in another relationship. The pain of it still stung.

But this was now. This was important. Astrid sucked her feelings into the pit of her stomach and forced herself to pay attention.

Bernie was still weighing the pros and cons of various materials. She and Aliyah got into a debate. No one else in the club voiced their opinion. To Astrid, Bernie looked like someone who was already in university. By the way she talked, it sounded like she was already there. Her long black hair was tied back in a ponytail, and she didn't seem like the sort who wore makeup. Her glasses framed dark eyes that were slightly tilted at the corners. Astrid wondered what it would look like if Bernie smiled.

Astrid forced her mind from wandering. She knew she was fairly good at math and the sciences.

But what was she doing in this group? Other than trying to get more extracurriculars for her college applications. She had relied on just doing well enough to get into a program. But now she really needed to impress. And these students were obviously really serious. Except for Karsyn.

Maybe it was feeling out of her league that made her want to stay. The past year, Astrid had started to see what she was made of. Robotics would not come easily to her, that was certain. Even following what Bernie was saying was hard.

But no one was going to come along and make things easier for her. She had to do it.

03 Building Something

THE NEXT WEEK, Astrid was looking forward to the bus ride out to UBC for some quiet time to look out the windows. But in the last class of the day, she got a text from her boss. They were short staffed at the yogourt place. Could she come right after school? Astrid was desperate to take all the shifts she could get. It wasn't like she was making big bucks, but everything counted. She texted back that she'd be there, even though it meant skipping one Robotics meeting. It was just the one and it was early days still. There would be plenty of time to make up for it over the next seven weeks.

It wasn't until the following Wednesday, a whole week later, that Astrid arrived at Robotics. This time, she was on time.

"Oh, it's you." Bernie sounded surprised. "I thought you dropped out."

To Astrid, Bernie might have sounded disappointed to see her, too. "Hey," Astrid said, taking a step back. "Yeah, sorry. I wasn't able to make it last week."

"Well, we already divvied up tasks. We set up a schedule and a target completion date." Bernie's tone was factual.

Astrid felt like she had already let Bernie down. And why did that bother her so much?

"Should I just go?" *It's like I'm getting shoved out the door anyway*, Astrid thought.

"You can stay," Bernie said. "But some of us take this very seriously."

"I can tell," Astrid said. "For what it's worth, I

didn't bail for nothing. I had to work."

"On schoolwork?"

"No. Froyo."

Bernie winced. Then she looked confused. It was written all over Bernie's face that, to her, this was not a valid explanation.

It wasn't like Astrid didn't agree. But she didn't have a lot of options. She was tempted to tell Bernie about her savings plan, how each paycheck put her one step closer to going to university. A year ago, university had been part of Astrid's plan. But then her dad lost his business and her mom lost her job. The family lost the house, the car, their savings, everything.

But Astrid had kept all this inside. She focused instead on squirreling away her froyo shop paychecks. She made sure to fly under the radar of anyone who might find her family's story tragic. She hated being tragic.

"It won't happen again," Astrid said. "I take this club seriously."

The truth was that she needed it.

♥ ♥ ♥

Astrid felt like she was in an alternate reality. Everyone else knew what they were doing. As much as she tried to be approachable and to offer help, no one needed her. She did the math in her head. What would happen if she ditched Robotics and took shifts on Wednesday nights instead? But then she thought about all the years she had spent building Lego sets with her dad. How she used to dream about the structures they'd make. How she wanted that again.

When she looked at the drawing on the whiteboard, Astrid wanted to see this project come together. Come alive. Even if it meant feeling out of place. It wasn't like she didn't feel that way at work, too. Or at school. Life had beaten her down. The real solution was to build something up.

Bernie got everyone busy with a challenge. Working in pairs, they had to come up with the sturdiest way to stack boxes. Astrid worked quietly with Ranj. Using foam bricks the size of couch cushions, they tried the obvious way of stacking higher and higher. But soon the problem became clear. If the point was to stack high, the robot would have to be sturdy. The higher the robot must lift the box, the sturdier the robot would need to be to keep the centre of mass relatively low. Astrid remembered trying to think like the Lego when building with her dad. Would that work here?

Astrid was distracted by the way Karsyn strode about the floor. It was like he was a teacher making the rounds while the rest of the class was working on an assignment. Wasn't he going to do any work? Or was the strutting his contribution to the project?

"Got it!" Karsyn exclaimed. It was loud enough to get everyone's attention. Before Bernie could call the end of the exercise, Karsyn began his theory. "We need to build something with big long arms that can grab all the boxes and stack them."

"Karsyn, other people are still working on their ideas," Bernie said.

"If it had big octopus arms, it could grab all the

boxes before anyone else gets a chance." It was like Bernie hadn't spoken. "We'd win for sure."

Aliyah said, "Karsyn, give others a chance, eh?"

In response, he paced around some more.

Finally, Bernie said the time was up. As she went around the room for their ideas, Astrid was bummed. They had all only managed to think like humans. She and Ranj had talked about creating railings to hold the boxes, but any monkey could come up with that.

Karsyn blurted, "What if we catapult the boxes into a huge net? Like basketball!"

"Part of the score is for innovation," Bernie said. "But points get taken off for dents and breakage."

"And the robot would have to bend over," added Aliyah. "That increases the chances that it will topple and fall."

"Instant disqualification," Bernie said.

Their comments only seemed to egg on Karsyn. "Yeah, but not if we create a really sleek structure."

Astrid didn't see what sleekness had to do with anything. And she hated admitting when people she didn't like had decent ideas. But in the vote, everyone else wanted the basketball idea.

"Okay, so we have the concept . . ." Bernie admitted. "Maybe . . . Or at least for now. So now we need to think about the how." She gave everyone a prompt to work on and they went back into pairs.

"I'm taking my girlfriend to see Billie Eilish this weekend." Karsyn was sitting close enough to Astrid that she could hear every word.

"Oh yeah?" Ranj said.

"Yeah, I was going to take her to Ariana Grande, but she wanted this concert. I got us box seats. Her Insta followers are going to go nuts when they see it."

"Does she have a lot of followers?"

"See for yourself," Karsyn said. He whipped out his phone.

"Whoa!"

Karsyn sat back and nodded. "She's not the easiest to satisfy. But I do it."

Astrid cringed. If he was talking about Ivy to get under her skin, he was doing a stellar job. It was true that Ivy paid a lot of attention to social media. But she was hardly a Kardashian. And it was true that she liked a good concert. But it wasn't like a big arena show was the only thing that got her interest. She remembered when she and Ivy had become fangirls of some buskers down at the beach. How much fun they'd had, how great the music was. How they had danced together in a crowd and felt free. If this guy thought it took box seats to impress Ivy, he would never know the side of Ivy that Astrid used to love.

04 Growing Up

ASTRID GOT READY for work. She put on the T-shirt with the yogourt logo, a cute smiley cup with a swirly hat. Her dad walked by her room in his own logoed work shirt. During the day, he worked on restoring the business that had gone bankrupt a year ago. Then he delivered food by bike for four hours every weeknight.

"I'm saving a bundle on my gym membership," he said with a smile. Leave it to him to put an annoying silver lining on their family's struggle. "Maybe we'll see each other later."

"Get lots of tips, Dad," Astrid said.

"You too," he said. They fist bumped each other.

She was all ready to go, but Astrid still had a few minutes before she had to leave. She sat down to do one more math problem. There was a unit test at the end of the week, so she was being all math, all the time.

She got super into the problem. It seemed to Astrid like time stood still.

But it didn't. *Uh oh.*

She was ten minutes late. She normally walked, took the bus, then walked some more. But now this was not a good plan. A taxi was too expensive. She grabbed her bike, even though it needed a tune up and the tire was flabby.

Between the helmet and her fast pedalling, she got to work sweaty and out of breath.

Lucy, the cashier, was pissy. "You're late, Astrid," she said. "What happened to you?"

Astrid tried to smooth down her hair. She could

feel how wet her scalp was and hoped she didn't have big wet pit stains, too.

"I'm so sorry I'm late. I'll just jump in right now."

"Great. I'm out."

So just like that, Astrid was in greeting customers with their towers of frozen yogourt topped with mochi and cereal and chocolate chips and marshmallows. She hoped the sight of her sweating like crazy wouldn't make them lose their appetite.

The problem was math. Once Astrid got into looking for an answer, she couldn't just give up on it. The equation she had selected seemed fast enough when she was doing it.

And now she had upset Lucy. Lucy was a couple of years older and in university. She usually looked out for Astrid. But as Lucy was leaving, Astrid overheard her telling their boss that it was a bad idea to hire high school students.

"Their minds just aren't developed yet," Lucy said. "They don't understand punctuality in the same way."

So it didn't surprise Astrid to find her boss standing

squarely in front of her.

"Maybe ten minutes is not a big deal in your world," he said. "But it is here. Next time, be on time."

"Okay," Astrid said. She mustered a smile. At the yogourt shop, smiles were mandatory. On the inside, she knew she'd screwed up. For some reason, it made her want to cry. In her old life, she used to be late all the time. It had been normal. In fact, Ivy was way worse than Astrid, and it had never been a big deal. But Astrid could see now that it actually was a big deal. The worst part was letting Lucy down.

With Lucy gone and her boss packing up, Astrid was left to deal with all the eager yogourt people alone. They were so impatient she could practically feel their *hanger*. And she knew it would be directed at her if she couldn't get them through the till fast enough. There was no sight more stressful than frozen yogourt melting into mush while she tried to weigh the cups and charge people. It really sucked when there was a rush. This was supposed to be a fun place, a fun experience. But tired parents and cranky kids could make it the worst.

A wave of loudness entered the shop. A big group of five showy guys. And that's when Astrid spotted Karsyn. *Not tonight*, she thought. It was hard enough being on the verge of tears with a long lineup. The last thing she wanted was to have to talk to Karsyn.

But for once, Karsyn's smugness worked in Astrid's favour. No *hi*. No *hello*. He didn't acknowledge her at all. Each guy grabbed a cup and started their swirling, while Astrid worked on the lineup.

Just then, Astrid's dad came in to collect an order. Her stomach sank. They'd done this many times before. But tonight, with Karsyn there, it was absolutely crucial that he be discreet. Her dad smiled at her. "Good evening."

"Hey," said Astrid, trying to be cool. "There's a chair at the back where some of the other picker-uppers wait. If you want, I can get you a lemonade."

He looked around. Astrid could see he was trying to figure out which person he was being hidden from. Then he shrugged and said, "Cool. Lemonade sounds pretty awesome right now."

"K." She gestured with her head for him to wait away from the crowd.

The farther he was away from her, the less likely he was to bust out a dad joke. Or to look at her in a way that would make her want to cry and get a hug and tell him how much she hated this job. Despite everything she said about it at home, she knew he could tell. Just like she could tell he was working every hour of every day because he was trying to get the whole family back on track.

She pointed him toward a dark corner. As soon as she could, she gave him a glass of lemonade and ran back to the lineup.

And then the moment came. Karsyn's crew came through the line.

"Oh, hey," Karsyn said, all cool. "Just put them all on one bill."

Astrid weighed all five of the tubs together and passed the machine to Karsyn. He tapped his gold Visa on the screen.

And they were gone.

"Friend from school?" Astrid's dad asked.

"Nah." Astrid was still watching the group. She didn't quite believe they had really left and that it was over.

"Okay. I'll stay out of it as long as I can get three pints of strawberry shortcake, one vanilla bean milkshake and a couple of mochi matcha explosions."

"Coming right up."

05 Thinking Like a Robot

ASTRID ARRIVED and found the workshop space empty.

"Sorry, I'm early," she said when Aliyah arrived with a fresh cup of coffee.

"No problem," said Aliyah. She headed for a desk that was piled with papers. "I'm going to keep working on this equation until group starts. Maybe even after group starts."

Being early was Astrid's new thing. She knew Lucy would approve. Astrid wanted to be here more than anyone. But if the past year had taught her anything, it was that wanting wasn't enough. You really had to make things happen. That was her philosophy at work, taking all those extra shifts. She already had a good chunk of cash saved.

"How are you doing, anyway?" Aliyah asked.

"Me?" It seemed like nobody had cared how she was doing for a long time. "Okay, I guess. Working a lot."

"Same here. Keeps us busy, right?"

"Yeah."

"You lived here your whole life?"

"Yep. I grew up in a house my grandparents bought decades ago. But we just moved to a different neighbourhood last year." Astrid did not want to give too many details. She turned the focus to Aliyah. "How about you?"

"Nah. I've only been here a year. From Toronto. I took this teaching gig at UBC. Good experience. Decent pay. But I have to say, Vancouver's a bit of a lonely town."

Astrid nodded. "Totally."

As she picked up a protractor, Astrid wondered if anyone in the club had the same pressures as she did. Obviously not Karsyn. But maybe Bernie or one of the other guys? No one talked about jobs.

"You're early," Bernie said as she bolted through the door.

"I often am," Astrid said. Then she felt that she sounded harsh. "How are you?"

Bernie grunted. "Well, it's been a week of trying to get the materials we need and it's impossible. And trying to wrap my mind around the physics of the idea we all voted on. I just don't think it's going to work."

"Okay," said Astrid. "So we change paths."

"Clock's ticking. We've already lost a bunch of time."

Astrid could feel the stress pouring off of Bernie. She wanted to help make it stop. "We'll get there."

"Don't try to put a positive spin on this. I'm the team captain. And our ship is sinking."

"So we come up with an idea for a lifeboat."

"We're nowhere. We have nothing. This thing's

got to be done in, like, six weeks. I heard that the other teams are already building. We don't even have a design." Bernie's voice trembled. Astrid could see she was flustered. Bernie put on her backpack as if she was going to walk out.

"Where are you off to?"

"I need some air. No, I need to focus."

Astrid took Bernie's backpack from her and tossed it on the ground. She kicked it under a desk where it would be hidden. "Aliyah, can we leave Bernie's stuff here for a minute?"

Aliyah nodded, without looking up from her work.

Astrid grabbed Bernie's hand.

"Where are you taking me? We have to work," Bernie insisted. "I don't really need air. I just need us to come up with a good idea."

"You need a reset," said Astrid firmly. "We're going for a run."

"Now? No way."

"Just a quick one. Trust me. You have to shake up this energy you're stuck in. You need to get out of your head for a minute."

It was drizzling outside. Not exactly a great day for it, but they ran. They took the brick path that followed the outside of the buildings.

First they ran in silence. Then Bernie started laughing. "You must think I'm a lunatic," she huffed.

"Little bit," Astrid said.

Bernie shrugged. "Can't hide the truth."

As they neared the door to the workshop, Bernie said, "Thanks. I didn't even know how much I needed that."

"We're a team," Astrid said.

Everyone was assembled by the time they walked inside. Bernie, who was out of breath, caught everyone up to speed. "Okay, so I've been doing nothing but calculations since the last time. And I just do not see how our idea can work. The math is not sound."

"It's a solid idea," Karsyn said.

"If you can defy the law of gravity," Bernie quipped.

He snatched the sketches and equations from

her hands. He looked through the papers quickly. "Lighter materials."

"Then we won't have the ballast support to hold up the boxes. It'll just fall over."

He looked at the papers again. "Heavier materials. We could build it out of metal. Then it would be very solid."

"The weakness is in the arm-like extension," Bernie said. "The problem with this idea is that it imitates humans. We need to think like robots."

Karsyn snickered. "*You're* a robot."

"I wish," said Bernie. "Do you know what I'd give to be a robot?"

Astrid chimed in. "Okay. Let's stop and breathe. Everyone, think like a robot."

"Humans can't think like robots," Bernie snapped. "That's the problem with being human." She sighed.

Astrid could see Bernie was annoyed. She hoped it wasn't with her. "Well, you're telling us we need to go back to thc drawing board. We need to clear our minds of what we've got in them. Maybe we should all just take a second to let go of this idea so we're ready to start from scratch."

Bernie let out a frustrated grunt. "I'm passing out paper. Work in pairs. Work alone. Breathe. Don't breathe. Whatever you need to do. But if we don't have a workable idea in the next hour, we are not going to be able to get this project done on time."

"I still say my idea works," said Karsyn, pouting.

"Then show me the math," Bernie said.

Aliyah jumped in. "Bernie is right. It won't work. Sorry, bud."

"But my tutor told me it would."

"Maybe you need a better tutor," Aliyah said. "Anyway, the ideas should come from you, not your tutor." She turned to the rest of the group. "What else you got? Y'all want to go into engineering, you need to be able to come up with more than one way to solve a problem."

With that, the group got quiet. Everyone was sketching and Astrid could hear quiet conversations going on around her. She tried to tune them out so she could think. It had become really hard for her to concentrate lately. All the interruptions of work and home and the busyness of her life got in the way. She valued having ten or fifteen minutes to just draw.

And that's when it hit her.

"Bernie?" Astrid motioned for the team captain to come over. "This might be way off. But what if, instead of arm-like extensions, we model it on those pallet lifters they use at warehouses? Instead of lifting the boxes, the robot goes in underneath like a spatula and picks them up. Then they get pulled upwards like stacking, but in reverse."

She showed Bernie her basic sketch. "I don't know how to do the math, but maybe you do."

Bernie looked at the drawing. "So what you're saying is we build it to take in the boxes from the ground. And then use a lever system to elevate them."

Astrid could tell Bernie was lost in thought as she worked her way through the idea. Bernie was quiet for so long that Astrid started to worry. Maybe Bernie thought Astrid was an idiot and was thinking of a nice way to tell her.

"I don't know why I didn't think of this," Bernie finally said. She rushed over to Aliyah's computer and plugged in some calculations.

Astrid followed. She didn't know the software that Bernie was using. She was trying her best to follow along anyway.

"Aliyah?" Bernie called her over. "What do you think of this?"

Aliyah hunched over the computer next to Bernie. They both got quiet. They whispered to each other. Much as she strained to hear, Astrid couldn't catch what they were saying.

"I think so," Aliyah said as she straightened up.

Then Bernie darted up and turned to face the group. "I think we've got it! Astrid, explain it."

Everyone looked at Astrid. She was terrified. What if she got this wrong? But if Bernie and Aliyah thought it was a good idea, maybe it was.

"Well," she said slowly. "What if we build

something with a solid base that takes the boxes in at the ground level? We could use a pulley system to lift the boxes from below rather than from above. That way, we might be able to stack more boxes and have a sturdy build that doesn't fall over."

She showed the drawing.

Some folks scratched their heads.

"So no arms?" Karsyn asked.

"No need," Astrid said.

"Arms are for humans," Bernie added. She looked at Astrid and smiled.

06 Sparks Flying

ASTRID SIPPED HER MORNING smoothie and a rare moment of peace washed over her. She looked at her calendar. Every day was booked with school, homework or work. She wouldn't have a day off to herself for at least a month. But she remembered how her dad urged her to think about where she'd be with her money goals by taking on all the extra work.

She looked at the empty pink delivery backpack waiting for him. She was impressed that he had kept it up all these months. He and her mom were doing everything they could to try to rebuild their lives. Her mom didn't exactly want to work evenings at Shoppers Drug Mart, but she did it. Sometimes Astrid thought about the way they used to live. The lavish parties her parents threw just a couple of years ago. The brunches. The fancy dinners. The vacations. All of that was gone. Two years ago, Astrid had fantasized about being an Instagram influencer. Now, no one would want what she had.

She went upstairs to the one small bathroom that the whole family shared. She wrinkled her nose at the towel her younger brother had left on the floor. She noticed her mom still had a couple of jars of face cream from their mother-daughter spa days. They wouldn't be having another one of those for a long time. And in a way, Astrid was relieved. It was luxurious, yes. But that life also came with a kind of pressure that she no longer felt.

Astrid used to try to keep up with people. Now everyone else was all so far ahead, it was like Astrid had dropped out of the race altogether. And maybe that was for the best. Her old crew would definitely not have encouraged robotics or math or physics. And if Astrid was being honest with herself, she had to admit it was kind of exciting to still be doing okay in those subjects. She knew that by the time they graduated from high school, most girls had lost interest in the sciences. Universities were full of science, math and engineering classes of mostly boys. It felt like a marvel that she was still going strong.

She put on some drug store eyeliner and called it done. This was a ponytail day for sure.

"Everything we need is here," Bernie said. "All of our building materials have arrived. But there's so much to do if we want to have this thing ready. We have five weeks. We'll need to meet at least twice a week if we want to finish. Maybe more."

Aliyah nodded. "I've been over the blueprints. The design is solid. But this is not going to be easy.

It's a completely different approach from other teams. To show you I'm committed, I've told my Dungeons and Dragons crew that my character is going to be frozen into an ice block for the next five weeks in a cocoon-like state and won't emerge until this robot is complete. So count me in."

"You're into D&D?" Bernie asked, sounding momentarily excited.

"I didn't say I was into it," Aliyah said with a smirk. "I never thought that would be a part of my life." She sighed and said, "Oh, Vancouver."

"I'll skip debate club," Karsyn offered.

Everyone else said they could commit to two or three times a week.

"Um," Astrid said. "I have to work. I'm already signed up for shifts." She pulled out her phone to show her calendar as proof.

Bernie's face dropped.

"I'll see what I can do," Astrid said, though she knew she didn't have a lot of options.

"That'd be great," Bernie said.

That night Aliyah walked them through the 3-D printer she'd been excited about from the start. They were able to get the base and the wheels done. Now they had a massive Roomba-like platform.

"Let's take it for a test drive," Bernie said as she placed it gently on the floor.

"It won't be able to take commands yet," Aliyah said. "Nothing's connected."

Karsyn moved to step on it.

"Don't!" Bernie commanded. "You're too heavy. You'll break it."

"It's supposed to be solid."

She rolled her eyes. "Not solid enough for you to stand on."

Bernie shot Astrid a look. Astrid noticed that she and Bernie had started to make eye contact when Karsyn was being annoying. She loved that they had an unspoken connection. On her side, it seemed to extend beyond being annoyed by Karsyn, too. Astrid felt drawn to Bernie in ways she could not quite explain.

Astrid couldn't tell if she liked Bernie or wanted to be like her. Bernie seemed like she was on a path to change the world. Astrid could picture her a decade older, being interviewed on the evening news about some invention that would solve some huge problem.

Bernie got down on the ground to examine everything. "I think we can start drilling this fitting here for the next piece."

"Can I get in on that?" Astrid asked. "I haven't used the drill yet. And I want to."

Bernie smiled at her. "Let's get the base up on the table."

Bernie helped Astrid lift it. It was surprisingly heavy for a short base with wheels.

Bernie put on eye protection and passed a pair of oversized clear plastic glasses to Astrid.

"Scoot over," Bernie said to Karsyn. She wedged herself between the two of them. Astrid was relieved to be standing next to Bernie. But she didn't want to crowd her.

"Okay," said Bernie. "We need to measure the

exact spot." She brought out the blueprints and made a quick calculation to get things to scale. Then she asked Karsyn to bring a ruler and a level. She made a tiny black dot with a marker. "Keep in mind that your drill bit needs to be smaller than the hole you want. You can expand the hole later. But if you make it too big the first time, you have to get rid of the whole piece and start over."

"It's like adding salt to a meal," Astrid said. "You can always add more, but you can't take it out." Astrid didn't know where that had come from. Or why she was suddenly nervous.

"Yeah. Like that." Bernie steadied Astrid's hand as she motioned toward the spot. She touched it lightly with the drill bit, then paused to make sure she had the right angle.

And then, just like that, Bernie went for it. Sparks flew. Little metallic curls dropped from the drill. The grinding of the two materials against each other was intense. Astrid was tempted to cover her ears, but she didn't want to be the only one.

The drill bit came out. Bernie tested the hole with the screw they would use. "Just a tad too snug," she said. She went in with the drill bit one more time, this time making the slightest adjustment with her hand. She tried the screw again. "There."

Bernie stepped back. "So three more like that on this side. Astrid?"

Bernie had made it look easy. Astrid was terrified of ruining the work that had already been done. But she had to try.

It took everything in Astrid to tune out the world. She wore ear protection even though Bernie hadn't. At first her hand was shaking out of nervousness. But she got it done. And then she did the other two.

"Nicely done," Bernie said.

It was the best Astrid had felt all week.

After everyone in the club had cleared out, Bernie and Astrid stayed to clean up.

"I'm glad you're getting the hang of it, Astrid," Bernie said. "It's nice to have another girl in here. It's been me and those guys for way too long. Especially Karsyn."

"What's his deal?" Astrid asked carefully. "He goes to private school?"

"Yep."

"Don't they have their own Robotics club?"

"Yeah. And he's in it."

"Isn't that a problem? I mean, he's double dipping. Trying to increase his odds of winning a competition."

"I guess." Bernie fiddled with her jacket.

"He could be a mole. He could be sabotaging our team to make sure his home team wins."

"I'm not sure high school robotics is that sinister," Bernie said.

Astrid tried to squash her feeling that Karsyn was a villain. "I don't like the idea of it either. I'm just saying it could be the case."

"I've known Karsyn for a long time. He wouldn't sabotage our group. He's annoying, but he's not evil."

Astrid had been hoping for a good gossip fest. She felt like she finally had an ally, someone who would get how it felt to be bound to someone like Karsyn. But Bernie was better than that, better than trash-talking.

07 Confessions

ASTRID WAS HYPED to meet the other clubs at the Robotics event. Bernie had made them sound fierce.

"This is just a tiny taste test of competition day," Bernie explained on the way in. Astrid was sipping her coffee. She could hardly believe she was giving up her Saturday morning sleep. But here she was at the Vancouver Convention Centre for eight a.m., after closing the froyo shop on a Friday night. Some things were just too good to miss. Like an outing with Bernie.

They walked into the big ballroom. There was a small crowd, chairs set up and a podium up front. A man fiddled with a screen.

"You've been to all of these things?" Astrid asked.

"Yep. Every event since I was in grade eight. This one is more about scholarships, but it'll be worth it for the guest speaker. His robot won the first year I came. Today he's back as a real mechanical engineer. Graduated from Waterloo."

"You talk about him like he's royalty."

"Robotics royalty." Bernie's little smile told Astrid that she enjoyed her bit of nerd humour.

Karsyn showed up with the same gang Astrid knew from the yogourt shop. They looked at her. She looked at them. She would have smiled if they had, but only if it was a real gesture of kindness. She was perfectly comfortable with them jumping to the conclusion that the only reason she smiled at the yogourt shop was because she had to. She watched coldly as they went to sit on the other side of the room.

"That group there is the X Factor," Bernie said.

"Karsyn's club from St. Michael's."

"Also known as my Sunday evening nightmare," Astrid said. "They hang out and eat frozen yogourt and leave a big mess for me to clean up. We have a whole routine going."

"Ugh."

"Truly. I hate my life."

"We've got the better club. Aliyah's awesome, for one thing. And you can't really compare even their super-funded lab with a real robotics workshop. That's why Karsyn double dips. I would too."

"You're surprisingly nice to him, you know." Astrid had to say it. "When he questions your authority and is annoying."

"What can I say? I'm used to him. We kind of grew up together. We're the only two who have been coming for this long. Yes, he's a rival. And I'm not going to tell him my best ideas. But I've learned to make peace with him."

Astrid compared Bernie's level of maturity with her own desire to throw yogourt all over Karsyn's school uniform. "But doesn't he get under your skin sometimes?"

Bernie looked down for a moment. It was like she was all in her head and didn't want to share what she was thinking. "I'm going to tell you something. But you have to swear you will not tell a single soul. Ever."

"Sure."

"No, like really swear it. It's embarrassing."

"Bernie, I swear. You can tell me anything."

"I was totally in love with Karsyn for, like, three years."

Astrid felt her eyebrows fly up. She had no poker face. She did her best to be cool, but all that came out was a choked "Really?"

"I know, it's silly. He has something though."

Astrid glanced over at Karsyn. He was shoving a muffin in his face. She looked back at Bernie.

"Yeah," said Bernie. "He can be a bit full of himself. But I used to think his confidence was kind of cool. And he really focuses when he wants to."

Astrid did her best to control her facial expressions.

"What changed? Like, how did you get over the crush?"

"Oh, that," Bernie got sheepish again. "Well, let's just say he made it clear there was no chance."

"*He* rejected *you*?" Astrid found this totally unthinkable. "Do you want me to kick him in the butt? Because I will."

"Nah, I'm over it."

"Good. He's not worth a second of your time. You've got a life of green lights ahead of you. You should enjoy every second."

"That's a really nice thing to say."

"It's the truth," Astrid said.

Bernie checked the time on her phone. They had a few minutes before things got started. "So why do you *not* like him?"

"You know how he's dating Ivy, right?"

"Yeah?"

"She used to be my girlfriend."

Bernie got stiff and adjusted her glasses. She fidgeted with the zipper on her hoodie. "I can see how that would be a challenge."

Astrid didn't know how to read Bernie's discomfort. She didn't think Bernie was a homophobe. But you could never really tell with people until you came out to them. They both shuffled around in their seats and Astrid wondered what was going on in Bernie's head.

The speaker came to the podium. He was the kind of guy who was smart but not good at public speaking. He was sweating and shaking. Astrid leaned back and took a sip of coffee. For a second, she got really excited about university. She had spent the last year busting her buns slinging yogourt and she would continue working over the summer, too. But now she pictured herself coming back to a robotics meet up and telling everyone about her journey. About attending lectures and becoming an engineer. And it would all be worth it.

The second the speaker was done, Bernie turned to Astrid. "Did he steal her? Did they cheat?"

"Nah," said Astrid. "There was this music festival that Ivy and I were supposed to go to. But I couldn't because . . . well, there was all this stuff going down with my family and I had to work. Ivy still went. She met Karsyn there."

"Were you sad about it?"

Astrid paused. "I mean, at the time."

"It must have been devastating. Not just to get dumped but then to watch her get together with someone else. With him especially."

Astrid was taken aback by Bernie's bluntness. "Wow. Way to home in on my sad situation." Then Astrid remembered to smile, so Bernie would know she meant it in an ironic way. The fact was, she was impressed with Bernie's directness.

"How long were you and Ivy together?"

"Six months."

"What was it like to have a girlfriend?"

"Okay," said Astrid. "Now you sound like a robot."

"I am a cyborg," Bernie said in a robotic voice.

"It was good, I guess," Astrid said, thinking about her time with Ivy. "There were certainly human feelings involved."

"Short circuiting. Short circuiting." Bernie pretended

her power source was causing her to break down.

Astrid wondered what was really going on. "You don't seem terrible with feelings, Bernie," said Astrid. "Why are you always saying you are?"

Bernie sat perfectly still. Like a broken robot. Astrid laughed. But as they stood up to leave, she said, "Clever. Avoiding my question like that."

"Cyborgs don't like talking about feelings."

Astrid nodded. "Okay, weirdo."

That night Astrid tried texting Ivy. She wanted to start a conversation. She wanted to let Ivy know that she had met Karsyn. She wanted Ivy to know what kind of guy she was dealing with. But the text didn't go through. She was still blocked. She hopped on social media. They weren't friends there anymore either. She thought about requesting a reconnection. But maybe that was a bad idea.

Astrid hated not being friends with Ivy. It was

silly. Just because they'd had this epic fight in front of a bunch of Ivy's friends . . . Astrid remembered and a raw wave of shame came over her. She had accused Ivy of being shallow. For caring more about the festival than about her.

Robots would never behave that way. They wouldn't be cruel for no reason. They really were better. Astrid thought it was smart of Bernie to wish to be a robot. What had feelings ever gotten her except for hurt?

She asked herself what she would do right now if she was a robot, or a part-robot. How would a cyborg handle this?

She sent Bernie a friend request.

08 Trying to Keep Up

ASTRID TOSSED HER BACKPACK on the floor beside her bed and flopped herself down on the mattress for five minutes. She thought about how life had changed around her in the past year. They had moved to this super tiny, dingy, smelly basement without any of their old stuff. Her big queen-sized bed was reduced to a sad, single mattress in a room she shared with her brother. Their lounge sofas, so big and comfy you could spend all day in them, were now some second-hand IKEA chairs her dad picked up for free from Craigslist.

Astrid used to dream of throwing parties. Now she wouldn't dream of even asking anyone for a ride home. What if they asked to use the washroom and she had to reveal the truth about how her family was living?

No matter. She was still in the game. Even if she was the smallest fish in a pond she hadn't realized was so big. The weird part was that, in the old days when times were good and she supposedly had no worries, she still worried a ton. Back then, her mind obsessed over what people thought of her, over her queerness, over her identity. Now she had no time for that. These days, her mind obsessed over how to keep up with every coordinated hour of every super-scheduled day. Her family's life falling apart had turned her into a person with high grades and a rapidly growing savings account. She never went to parties, like she had thought she would in her final year of high school. But at least she had a sense that things would get better next year.

And until then, the one thing she could count on feeling good about was Robotics.

She got a text from her boss. He was in a panic because someone had called in sick. If it had been any other day of the week, Astrid would have made it work. But Robotics was too important.

When Astrid walked into the workshop, Bernie was in full-on fire mode. She had already built the core. Astrid loved watching her concentrating on something. She looked so powerful. Confident.

"What happened here?" Astrid teased. "We leave you alone for two days and the project is done?" She plunked her canvas bag down on the table.

"Not done . . . just . . ." Bernie looked at it. Then she looked at Astrid and sat up straight. "I guess it is a lot closer."

Astrid nodded. "How often do you come here?"

"As often as Aliyah will let me. That's, like, five

days a week." Bernie shifted in her seat. She sounded almost embarrassed. Astrid couldn't understand why. She thought Bernie's dedication was really cool. But she didn't say that.

Astrid put down her umbrella and coat. "Can I help?"

"I was just tinkering."

"But you're always working. What can I do?"

"I was going to run the code and see if the first application can do what we need it to." Bernie looked back and forth between the computer and the piece she'd been fixated on when Astrid came in. She seemed flustered and let out a small grunt.

"Maybe you should go and come back when the club starts." Bernie said.

"Really?" Astrid felt a pang. Bernie didn't want her here.

"I'm just . . ." she kind of grunted again. "I'm sorry. I'm not used to people asking if they can help. It's a mixed thing. You know?"

Astrid shook her head. "What's wrong with

people offering to help?"

"I like it when people see what needs doing and pitch in. But when someone can't see what needs to get done it interrupts my flow. I don't like having to stop what I'm doing to come up with a task."

Astrid's stomach sank. She didn't want to be a burden on Bernie. She hadn't even known she'd overstepped some kind of unspoken boundary. "I'm sorry. I'll go."

"You don't have to."

"Obviously you like it more when I'm not here."

Now Bernie let out a sigh. "That's not it. If you'd noticed that I'm in the middle of running code so we can try testing the core function later on, you'd know that this step involves a lot of waiting."

Astrid got annoyed. "I'm not a mind reader. And I'm not a mechanical engineer like you." She put her coat back on and picked up her bag and umbrella. "See you in twenty-two minutes."

"You really don't have to go."

"I don't want to stay."

Bernie looked at her watch. "See you in twenty-one minutes, then."

Astrid went to walk quietly along the pathway that connected the brick buildings. She wanted to cry. She was tempted to quit. *Just get on the bus, go home, never think about this competition or the team captain ever again,* she told herself. How devastating to think that Bernie saw her as a pain in the butt, like someone she needed to babysit by coming up with a task for. She'd come to feel like Bernie was the person she most looked forward to seeing. But that's not how Bernie felt about her.

Astrid thought about Ivy, how she hadn't felt good enough then either. But that was on a whole different level. Astrid wasn't cool enough, didn't care as much about her status. And when things went badly for her family, she couldn't keep up with Ivy at all anymore. Focusing on school seemed like the only logical way out of that mess.

And she hadn't really been interested in anyone again until now. And Bernie pretty clearly did not like her.

Her boss texted her again, this time even more desperate. If she hadn't had that fight with Bernie just now, she would say no to her boss. But every shift she took was one step closer to securing next year.

Besides, she didn't know how to face Bernie.

Astrid spent days being down on herself for choosing work over facing her fears that day. She could have just gone back to the club. Why did she need to make some kind of point? It was clear that Bernie didn't care, since she never reached out.

Astrid found Bernie infuriating. And mysterious. The more Astrid thought about how Bernie had pushed her away, the more she thought there must be more to the story. People don't do that for no reason. And then she thought about how someone like Bernie probably didn't have the easiest time walking through the world. Whip smart but kind of under-the-radar. It didn't score you big points in high school.

Astrid thought about texting Bernie to say she was sorry she had left or to explain herself. But she couldn't get the words right without sounding like some kind of grovelling suck-up.

It was Saturday, her one day off. She had boatloads of homework, but she had an idea. Astrid sent a text off to Bernie.

Hey. What are you doing today? Want to study together?

Already at the library. Fifth floor. Downtown.

On my way.

09 It's a Date

ON THE BUS on the way to the library, Astrid thought about how relieved she was at the speed of Bernie's texts. That told her she wasn't completely nuts for reaching out. After all, Bernie wasn't exactly the easiest person to get to know.

When she got to the concourse, she picked up two medium mochas from Blenz. She carried them in a tray in one hand, with all her other belongings in the other. She was all set to hunker down for a while.

As she went up the escalators, she felt sweat beads forming along her hairline. There was tension in her stomach as she wondered if this was a good idea. Was she ready to get to know Bernie outside of Robotics? It had been cool when they went for the lecture, but that was different. That was about robotics. This was just hanging out. And to Astrid, hanging out was a big deal. She hadn't done much of that since the Ivy days. And that was dating.

Oh my God, she thought just as she reached the fifth floor. *Is this a date?*

She looked at the mochas she was carrying. Maybe she should stash them somewhere. Or maybe Bernie was sitting with a big group of people. Then it would be obvious it was a friend thing. Astrid knew she was overthinking everything. It got worse with each step she took toward the carrels. She walked around, looking for Bernie. She scanned the section by the windows, where the misty grey weather cast a beautiful cool tint over everything. And there was Bernie's unmistakable ponytail. It was also easy to tell it was Bernie because she was hunched over, concentrating. Pretty much everyone else their age was slouched back napping or checking their phones.

"Hey," Astrid said quietly.

"Oh." Bernie turned around. "Hi."

"Caffeine?" That sold it as a drink of utility, not some kind of thoughtful gesture.

"Sure. Thanks." Bernie took the tray so Astrid could put her stuff down. "I saved this spot for you." It was the carrel right next to her.

"Great." Astrid plunked down her stuff. Did sitting next to each other mean something different from sitting across from each other? "What are you working on?"

"Physics," Bernie said. "You?"

"Math."

"Nice."

Astrid nodded.

With that, Bernie went back to what she was doing. She disappeared into her own world.

Astrid thought it was really something to feel like

this. She was spending time with someone who could see that studying at the library was actually kind of a good time for her, even if there was a lot of homework. She got to work and time stood still. Like Bernie, she got caught up in her own thing for so long that when she finally took a sip of her mocha it was cold. Still delicious, though.

"So, uh, what happened to you the other day?" It was Bernie who broke the silence. "You didn't come back."

"I took a shift last-minute."

"You work a lot, don't you?"

"Every chance I get." But Astrid did not want to talk about work. Or why working was necessary. "I'm sorry I bailed on Robotics, though. I really missed it."

Bernie smiled. "Yeah, we missed you, too." Then she returned to her textbook. Astrid could tell that was the end of that conversation. But she was pleased that Bernie just said that. It made her insides feel squishy.

Hours passed. Now and then, when stuck on a problem, Astrid would glance over and see Bernie touching the eraser tip of her pencil to her chin. Astrid thought the gesture totally suited everything about her.

There was an announcement that the library would be closing in fifteen minutes. They started packing up.

"I'm kind of hungry. Want to grab dinner?" Astrid asked. The second the words were out of her mouth, she was nervous. If it hadn't felt like a date before this — and it kind of had — dinner would turn it into one.

"Actually, it's takeout day at home," said Bernie. "Every Saturday, my family gets takeout. You're welcome to come."

"Sure," Astrid said. "I'd like that."

"You can meet Chip."

"Is that your brother?"

"Nope."

"Dog?"

"Chip is the robot I built last year."

"I'm in," Astrid said.

Just before leaving the concourse, they put on their rain jackets and unfolded their umbrellas. Even though it was May, there was a downpour. They ran, dodging raindrops, the few blocks up to Granville to catch the bus.

They walked from the bus stop to Bernie's house in Mount Pleasant. Astrid looked around the familiar tree-lined streets. She remembered when her family lived not too far from here. Now she saw it differently than she had then, as a very beautiful place to grow up. They walked in silence. With anyone else but Bernie, it probably would have felt awkward. But Astrid was comfortable with neither of them saying anything.

"Sometimes people think I don't like them, when actually I do." Bernie paused for a second. "I've stopped trying to understand how people work."

"Really? You're just not going to try to understand people?"

"I prefer machines."

"You've made that clear."

"I'm trying to tell you that I feel bad you left the other day. In the future, you don't need to leave. If it's not clear how you can help, it's okay."

"I'm really glad you said that. I wasn't sure what to do that day. That's why I took the shift last minute."

"Did I hurt your feelings?"

"A little."

"I didn't mean to."

"I can tell."

Bernie's house was an old A-frame wooden home with a porch and big lilac bushes out front. They were budding, almost in bloom, and Astrid could smell the beginnings of summer. She was starved for the warmth, even though spring rain was kind of her favourite.

Bernie's room like that of every young mad scientist. She had posters of Einstein and Richard Feynman and Neil deGrasse Tyson on the wall, as well as movie posters of *Chappie*, *Wall-E* and *Star Wars*. There was a dresser in the corner. In most girls' rooms, it would be covered with makeup and hair products. Here, the surface was cluttered with parts. From far away it looked like Bernie collected specialized Lego sets and all the strange bits that didn't fit littered the top of the dresser. But on closer look, Astrid could see that the bits and pieces were metal. *They must leftovers from Bernie's builds*, she thought.

"This is Chip," Bernie said. She held up a robot the size of a loaf of bread.

"Pleased to meet you," the robot said.

"You as well," said Astrid, smiling.

"Chip, sort through my pencil case." Bernie put Chip on her bed on top of a textbook. Next to the book, she put another textbook to create a smooth surface. She opened her backpack and pulled out her pencil case. She placed a handful of mixed pens and pencils on the textbook next to Chip. Chip started to place the pens in one pile and the pencils in another.

"Wow." Astrid was amazed. "How did you do it?"

"It took a long time. But I figured out how to get Chip to recognize wood and plastic. He still short circuits with bamboo chopsticks. I don't like to do that to him."

Astrid smiled. "Of course you don't."

Robots don't have feelings, yet here was Bernie trying to be mindful of how she treated Chip. Astrid shook her head at the idea. All the strange and lovely complexities that were Bernie.

10 Knowing Your Priorities

"DINNER'S HERE!" Bernie's mom called from downstairs.

Bernie and Astrid came down the creaky wooden stairwell. The sound was as familiar to Astrid as home. They got to the front hallway just in time for Astrid to take in the full view of the open front door.

This was a full-on panic situation.

"Oh, hey, Dad," Astrid said.

Her dad had the grey and pink square backpack in his arms. He was passing trays of food to Bernie's mom.

"Astrid, what are you doing here?" he asked. He looked as surprised to see her as she was to see him.

"This is Bernie," Astrid gestured at her friend. "From Robotics."

"Oh, hi," he said. "I'm Arne."

Bernie's mom said her name was Sue and her dad introduced himself as Sinclair.

"Okay, well I've got more people waiting for dinner," Astrid's dad said, mercifully cutting things short. "I'll see you at home later."

"Bye, Dad."

Astrid and her dad waved at each other like it was nothing. Like this sort of thing happened all the time.

The door closed behind him. Astrid felt strangely cut off from the situation that had started and ended so fast.

"Bernie, would you set the table?" Bernie's dad asked. He had a sweet, kind-of-goofy smile. Astrid thought he looked like the actor Randall Park.

"Can I help?" Astrid offered.

"You can put out water glasses and fill the water

jug," said Bernie's mom, an intelligent looking woman wearing artsy glasses and a colourful scarf around her neck.

"Okay," Astrid said. She wanted to explain about her dad, but she didn't know what to say. And she was surprised to find that it was okay. If she was anywhere else it might have been awkward, but here it didn't seem like a big deal.

"Your dad was pretty sweaty," Bernie said. "I should have offered him a glass of water."

"He's okay. He brings his water bottle everywhere," Astrid said.

When they sat down at the table, Bernie's mom said, "So, Astrid. What's your favourite subject?"

"Math," she said. "Well, and History and English. But I think next year I'm going to focus on Math. Maybe take some foundational engineering classes."

"Astrid was the one who came up with the idea of stacking the boxes from the bottom," Bernie said. "And using a lever-pulley to crank them up."

"Yes, you told us that," Bernie's dad said. He turned to Astrid. "Very clever."

Astrid felt honoured that she had come up in conversation.

Upstairs in Bernie's room, Astrid finally felt able to talk to Bernie about it. "You know, a year ago I would have been so embarrassed if I was at a friend's house and my dad was working as a delivery guy."

"It looks like hard work," Bernie said.

"It is. He comes home exhausted and goes right to bed. Then he spends all day working on getting his business back."

"So that's nothing to be ashamed of. That's actually really cool."

"It is, isn't it?" Astrid said. "And before we lost it all, I wouldn't have thought that. I guess I was more like Karsyn. Hanging around not being super nice to servers, not really taking school all that seriously because I figured it would work itself out somehow. Now I know I have to carve my own path. I'm on my own with it."

"It's not a bad thing to know your priorities," Bernie said. "How did your family lose it all?"

"My dad had to close up shop for a few months. But he couldn't stand to lay off people. It's a family business and his employees had kids, so he kept payroll the same, and people worked from home. But it just didn't work. My mom started yelling and screaming about it, saying we'd lose our house. And we did. When all that was going down, she lost her management job at a non-profit because of budget cuts. We used to live in a big old house my grandparents bought in the thirties. Now we're renting over by Joyce station."

"Oh. Is that hard?"

"No. I mean, it's cramped. We have maybe ten percent of the space we used to have. We had to use my RESPs to survive. We literally have nothing. That's why I work like crazy now. If I don't, no uni for me next year."

"Oh. I'm sorry I made an issue about your work."

"No, it's okay. I could have told you the whole story. But it's good you know now. I've never actually told anyone before."

"You find it embarrassing."

"You know, I'm surprisingly okay telling you. I feel like you're not judging me. But my old circle, they wouldn't understand. There's no way. They were all so caught up in the usual high school crap that I'm actually kind of glad to be away from them."

"I've never known what it was like to be like that. What was that like?"

"Overrated. For me anyway. I couldn't keep up with them. Like, at all. Everything they wanted to do was stuff I couldn't do anymore. And none of them even asked me why I couldn't go out with them anymore. They were fine to just go on without me." Astrid started tearing up. "I used to think I belonged in that group, like we were going to be friends forever. But I went on one shopping day downtown with the girls. I was the only one who didn't buy anything. They didn't say anything, but I could tell. And then we went to dinner and I didn't eat and they were weird about it. And then the next weekend we were supposed to be going to an escape room together and there was just no way I could afford it, so I just said I didn't feel like it. And that was pretty much the last I heard from them."

"Was Ivy part of that?"

"No, I knew Ivy from a queer dance thing. Ivy and that group didn't get along so great. But mostly because Ivy was more indie and into music that my old crew didn't care about. She dressed differently and had, like, black and chrome nails."

"They didn't like her because of that?"

"I think Ivy didn't like them for liking Pacific Centre so much. But who knows. All of them liked Sephora. I don't know how many hours I've been forced to browse in that store. And all I could do was ask for samples." Astrid rolled her eyes as she thought back on it. "You know, it's really no wonder I'm happier now."

"You are?"

"Yeah. It's strange. I feel like I dodged something. Like I could have wasted a bunch of years being caught up in all the wrong stuff. Don't get me wrong. I was devastated when it was all taken away. But I was more sad for my family than about losing my friends."

"I think your family will bounce back. If they're anything like you, they probably know what's most important."

"You know, when this first happened, when they repossessed the house and cars and seized the bank accounts, it was right before Mother's Day. My mom wailed like someone had died because we couldn't do our annual mother-daughter spa day with high tea at the end. She cried all day. I was kind of okay without it. To tell you the truth, it was never for me. I never liked that girlie stuff all that much."

"I don't either."

"I know," Astrid said. There was that smile on her face again. "I can tell."

11 *Call Out*

ASTRID WAS BUSY with a circuit board, trying to hold everything still so Bernie could connect some wires. The two were quietly getting things done. Astrid was admiring Bernie's persistence. She found herself questioning the magnetism she felt between them. Was it just her? Or did Bernie feel the pull, too?

Astrid brushed off the sensation as nothing more than nerves and circumstance. Working so closely together, on something so exciting, there were bound to be feelings. But the best thing to do was stuff them down and focus on the work. Wasn't that the Bernie way? Astrid wondered if Bernie was doing that right now.

Karsyn was across the room, but loud as ever. He was talking with Azi.

"My girlfriend *used to be* one of these," Karsyn said holding up a female-to-female connector.

Azi laughed in a polite way that made it clear he was uncomfortable.

Astrid flinched. "What?"

"I wasn't talking to you," Karsyn said.

"Good, because it sounded like you were implying that Ivy is no longer queer just because she's dating a guy right now."

"So?"

"So you haven't heard of the miracle of bisexuality?"

Karsyn shrugged. "I don't think she's that way anymore."

Astrid got up from where she was seated and walked over closer. The blood coursed through her veins.

She could feel her chest rise. "And what *way* is that?"

"You know. Queer."

"Oh I *do* know. And I also know you're out of line talking about her like that. You don't know who she's going to date after you. You don't define her."

"You're just pissed because you couldn't hang onto her."

The entire room had gone silent. Aliyah jumped in. "Folks, let's change the tone in here."

Astrid was about to let Karsyn have it. But Aliyah was right. This wasn't the time or place. Besides, she could take it too far. Never had she wanted to punch someone in the face as much as she did right now. Everything in her body was telling her to do it. It was only through willpower and reason that she restrained herself.

Breathing, reminding herself to be cool, Astrid walked back to her workstation. Bernie looked uncomfortable. For someone who claimed not to have feelings, she sure didn't like conflict.

Astrid wanted to let it go. She did. Breathing,

breathing. "Just so we're all clear, sexuality is a spectrum." She said it loud enough for the whole room to hear.

"Yeah, and some people are straight," Karsyn replied.

Astrid couldn't help herself. "And some straight people are attracted to some bisexual people. And it doesn't change the sexuality of either of them."

She *really* wanted to let it go. Breathe. But Karsyn was making this personal. He was trying to erase her time with Ivy. Trying to tell her it didn't matter. It stung that Ivy had completely dropped her, and that she'd hurt Astrid's feelings. That she'd broken Astrid's heart. One thing was sure. It was between Astrid and Ivy. Their relationship had nothing to do with Karsyn.

"It's also okay to think you're gay and then realize you're not." Karsyn wouldn't let it go.

"That's highly unlikely," Astrid said. "Statistically improbable. But tell yourself whatever you need." She knew it was below the belt. But so was everything he said, and Astrid was sick of being nice. This shot was payback for all the times she had to hold it together at the yogourt shop. She had been holding it for too long.

"She's super into *me*," Karsyn said.

"Then respect her for everything she is," Astrid snapped.

Karsyn looked like he was going to boil over.

Aliyah literally stepped between them. "Why do I feel like I'm a bouncer?" she said, trying for a light tone.

Astrid and Karsyn stared each other down. Astrid could have gone for it. It would have felt good to lay into him. Not that she was much of a fighter. She hadn't scrapped with anyone since elementary school, and that was mostly for fun. Right now she felt like a bull. Karsyn's biphobia was the red cape she wanted to fling herself toward. She wanted to smash his ignorance into a thousand pieces.

"Let's step outside," Aliyah said to Karsyn.

"Why do I have to go?" he argued. "She's the one being hostile."

"She'll get her turn with me after you," Aliyah said. She was stern, like a boss.

Karsyn glared at Astrid as he followed Aliyah outside.

Bernie looked like she was trying to look busy. She had her nose buried in some calculations. The faces on the rest of the club showed the same discomfort. Everyone looked like the shocked emoji with the perfectly round eyes.

"Sorry," Astrid said. She was not sorry that she called Karsyn out, only that she disrupted the club. "I will never stand by and let a straight person define what's queer and what's not."

Her words hung in the air. She wasn't sure if the rest were mad at her, or if some of them agreed with her. One thing she'd learned was that she had to do what felt right. Even if it meant standing alone.

When Karsyn and Aliyah came back in, Aliyah grabbed Astrid. They went into the hall together.

"What's up?" Aliyah asked when they were out of earshot.

"You heard him," said Astrid. "He was being a giant homophobe. I had to say something."

"Astrid, I agree with holding people accountable. But you have to think about the group dynamic. It doesn't help to square off with him like that. It's not fair to the rest of the group to make them choose sides."

"But he makes me so mad."

"I get that. Believe me. But think about your own future and your own professional conduct. Don't let the haters get you down. Let them sink their own ships. Does that make sense?"

It did. Except sometimes it felt to Astrid like Karsyn was on a yacht. And she was paddling around in one of those inflatable rubber boats kids used at the beach. But she did understand the bigger picture. She couldn't let him ruin her game. She'd come so far. It would cost her too much.

As they walked back into the workshop, Astrid thanked Aliyah. She told her she appreciated the way she helped her tap into the better part of herself.

Aliyah addressed the whole club. "I've been

running groups like this for a lot of years now. It's always been a group of young enthusiasts. They don't always agree. That goes without saying. But I've never had to kick out anyone yet and I hope I never have to. We can all stand to improve the way we think about our words and how they land on others. And we all need a chance to improve. Homophobia, racism, ableism, sexism . . . none of that stuff flies in here. Okay, back to work."

And with that, a humbled Karsyn returned to his chair.

The night was tense. Only the most necessary words were spoken. But somehow the group got more than usual done.

It wasn't until Astrid was putting on her rain gear to leave that Ranj caught up with her.

"I'm glad you said something," he said.

"Thanks," Astrid said.

"That guy has always gotten away with saying things the rest of us would never say or think."

"I felt like I caused a scene."

"Nah. See you next time."

On the 99 on the way home, Astrid replayed the interaction over and over in her mind. She decided that Ranj was on her side. And that, even if she couldn't say it, so was Bernie. And Aliyah. And probably Azi, too, even if he didn't want to get involved.

Her dad had always told her that success was the best revenge. Instead of slugging Karsyn in a high school Robotics club, what if she took her future so seriously that she went into robotics? What if she came up with something amazing and years later they'd meet randomly? It would be obvious that she'd won. Yeah, that was the way to think about it.

12 Turning It On

THE NEXT MEETING, Karsyn didn't show up. Astrid assumed it was her doing. She wasn't sure if it was a failure or a triumph for her.

Bernie's pep talk was short and simple. "Okay, people. We are getting dangerously close to competition day. And we don't really know whether we have a working robot or a big heap of junk. Let's get our parts assembled."

They'd all been looking forward to assembly day.

This was when all the little parts would come together. They would finally see if they fit properly and would work off the circuit board.

"Astrid, let's get you on drilling," Bernie said.

"Okay." Astrid grabbed for a white lab coat and began to gear up. She put on goggles. Hearing protection dangled around her neck and everything.

This had become Astrid's favourite part, working the machinery. It conjured images of a metal shop, of welding and of working with raw materials to create something great. It was the ultimate feeling of being a mad scientist in a lab, free to unleash some boldness into the world.

She had also found that doing stuff in front of Bernie was very different for her. When Astrid had first joined the club, she was scared but happy to be there. But her feelings for Bernie had filled her with doubt. Daydreaming about Bernie was a secret, one she wasn't sure she could ever share. Maybe Bernie was a nice good straight girl. And Astrid was thinking about her in ways she shouldn't be.

"So let's get holes here and here," Bernie instructed. She placed the shaped sheet metal on Astrid's station.

Astrid was aware that Bernie was standing a little too close. Was that on purpose?

"Okay," Astrid said again. She pulled on the heavy-duty orange ear protectors that looked like headphones on steroids. Now she was in a vacuum, unable to hear the world around her. She welcomed the barrier. It was like stepping into her own cocoon. It didn't keep her from feeling self-conscious, but at least she could pretend to concentrate.

She worked on getting the holes to be just right, a hair tighter than they needed to be. When Bernie came to inspect her work, she took off her hearing protection. It was like coming back naked to the exposed world. She wasn't sure she liked it. Better to stay inside the quiet landscape of her mind where it was safe.

"Beautiful," Bernie said. Astrid wanted to be able to brush it off. She hated compliments. But from

Bernie, the approval made her squirm. "Why don't you sand the edges of this piece? Then we can fit it onto the back and screw it in place."

Astrid gave Bernie a thumbs-up, then took the sander to the rough edges. It was exciting to be at the stage where their robot might actually carry weight. If this part succeeded, they had the foundation of a functional machine. With each piece the excitement grew.

She was turning the sheet of metal when it happened. It was a just small nick, but there was a lot of blood. She was so shocked she let out a sound.

Bernie came running. She took a quick glance at Astrid's hand. "It's okay. I'm trained in first aid." No sooner did she run for the first aid kit than she was back.

Astrid sat looking down at her hand. The cut was to the stretchy skin that connected the thumb to the hand, like the webs on a duck's feet. Astrid had received many small nicks and cuts in her life, but this was the first time she noticed that area.

Bernie put on blue gloves and opened an alcohol wipe. She placed the tiny wet white square onto the wound and held it in place. Hard.

"It's okay," Astrid offered, putting out her hand to where Bernie was holding her hand. "I got it."

"No, no. It's better if I put some pressure on it. Stay still and it'll all be good."

Astrid settled in. She liked this. No question. The sight of the blood had scared her. But Bernie taking charge felt right. Astrid was in good hands. Not to mention that those hands were pressed to hers. Sure, it was to stop the bleeding. But it was at least a little bit dreamy.

Astrid glanced up to see Bernie looking right at her. Their eyes met and Bernie said, "I know the exact right bandage to use in this case."

Astrid smiled. Of course Bernie knew the right bandage.

"Check it out," Bernie said. "It looks like a butterfly. It makes it so that you can move your hand around, but the bandage stays on. Watch."

Bernie intently peeled the bandage from its wrapper and applied it to the cut. She smoothed down all the adhesive corners of the butterfly's wings, and firmly patted it down. Astrid felt tingles everywhere.

"All done."

"Thank you," Astrid said. What else could she say? *Keep going?* No, that wouldn't be cool.

"Now sit here for a moment with your hand raised," Bernie ordered. "You don't want to cause sudden blood flow."

"No." Astrid shook her head. "I definitely don't want that."

Astrid watched Bernie get back to work. She saw that Bernie had no clue how adorable she could be. Bernie probably had no idea how Astrid felt about her.

The trouble was that someone like Bernie was hardwired to do the right thing. She'd have given first aid to absolutely anyone, whether they were a team member or a random person on the street. This much Astrid knew. And that meant it was dangerous to read too much into anything. Bernie didn't come to Astrid's rescue because Astrid was special. Bernie did it because she would have done it for anyone.

Astrid sat there, her hand in the air like someone with questions that would never be answered. Her mind wandered back over all the things she and Bernie had done together. Going to the lecture. The day at the library. The time at Bernie's house. She questioned what it all might mean. If Bernie was so nice, maybe she would have invited anyone over.

Astrid watched Bernie glide around, connecting one person's work to another's. This was her jam. Building something. Getting a whole team to create something bigger than the sum of its parts. A self-stacking robot — pretty incredible. A few weeks ago, Astrid barely knew what a robot could do. And now, here she was, part of it all. The crew was almost ready to hold the core pieces together. Even with her little accident, soon they'd get to see whether they could turn this thing on.

13 *Life*

THE CIRCUIT BOARD lit up.

"We have life!" Bernie exclaimed.

"Not exactly life," Ranj corrected.

Bernie rolled her eyes.

"Don't be a buzzkill, Ranj," Astrid scolded. "Can't you see she's having a Frankenstein moment?"

Bernie looked right into Astrid's eyes and smiled.

Azi and Ranj shook their heads, looking at each other.

Astrid's phone buzzed. She wasn't about to let anything or anyone interrupt her. It was probably just her mom. But she couldn't resist taking a glance.

It was Ivy.

Astrid wanted to pay complete attention to the robot and everything around her. But now she needed to know what was up. She stole a moment and slipped away. She hoped it looked super casual. The truth was she would rather have not taken the call.

Astrid went outside and ducked under a tree. She called Ivy back.

Ivy was already on the offense. "What the hell did you say to Karsyn?" she barked. "He's been super weird. He's laying all kinds of pressure on me that he didn't used to. I know it's got something to do with you. With something you said."

"What kind of pressure?" Astrid racked her brain. "Sex?" *What a jerk*, she thought.

"Yeah sex. What the hell do you guys talk about in Robotics anyway?"

"Uh . . ." What was Astrid supposed to say?

Ivy was clearly in no mood to hear about Karsyn's misguided ideas about sexual orientation. About Ivy.

"Well, stop it, whatever it is. Get your nose out of my business. Let me handle Karsyn my own way."

With that, the conversation was over.

Astrid got up from the wet rock and smoothed down her clothes. She found a crumpled tissue in her pocket and ran it beneath both eyes. No point in sitting out here. She went back inside.

She found Bernie literally doing a happy dance. It was the dorkiest, cutest thing Astrid had ever seen.

On the 99, Astrid looked out at the city through the wet blanket of rain. She thought about everything she had gained, not everything she had lost. She looked at her phone again, staring at the number that showed how long she'd talked with Ivy. One minute, seventeen seconds. Just a tiny dip into her old life. It was enough to show that Astrid did not belong there anymore.

Ivy could keep her drama.

As for Karsyn, he had pretty much sucked all along. So none of this was surprising.

She got home to a rare sight. Her brother was in the big chair as usual. But both her parents were plunked down on the couch watching TV and eating . . .

Could it be true? "Takeout?" Astrid breathed. She was completely gobsmacked. It had been so long.

"Yeah," her dad said. "Get this. I went to deliver it but no one answered the door. I did another drop off and came back. Still nothing. The guy from the restaurant said I should just keep it. Or throw it out. So, butter chicken for everyone."

"We're eating someone else's dinner?" her brother asked. He looked at the food on his fork.

"There's nothing wrong with it."

"I'm not asking any questions," Astrid said. She grabbed a plate from the cupboard and helped herself. This was what dinner used to look like most nights of the week. Cardboard boxes all over the dining table. Of course, back then, the table was a lot bigger.

She sat down and ate with her family.

"What are you both doing off at the same time?" she asked around a mouthful of basmati rice.

Her mom looked at her dad and back at Astrid. "Shoppers was dead. My shift supervisor said I could leave early. I texted your dad to tell him, and he told me about dinner."

"Best thing that's happened in a long time," her dad said. "Didn't I tell you? We'll turn this ship around."

It felt decadent to be eating a plate of delicious butter chicken. Astrid sat down with her parents in front of the TV. There was an episode of *Glow* on. Perfect. A show about transformation.

Later that night, Astrid was in her room studying when her dad came in.

"How's things, kid?" he asked.

She shrugged. "Kinda got a lot on my plate these days. But okay, I guess. You?"

"Tonight was just what I needed. You know, we haven't had a family dinner in months."

"Yeah. We're all busy."

"Well this one will keep me going for a while. It reminds me of what I want us to get back to. We might never get the firm back or the old house. But I think we can manage to not all be working at the same time at some point."

"It was nice, Dad."

"Astrid, it can't be easy on you. I hope you're not ashamed when we see each other at work. Or, you know, the other day at your friend's place."

"Ashamed? Dad, I'm proud of you."

Her dad's eyes teared up. "I feel like I failed you all. Big time."

"It wasn't your fault."

"That's not what your mom says when she takes all those extra shifts." He sat in her plastic desk chair. "We can't support you in the way we always said we would. And that sucks."

"I'm working on the scholarships. And saving every paycheck. It'll be okay, Dad."

"How'd you get to be so grown up?" He hugged her.

"That friend of yours the other day . . . is she from school?"

"No, that's Bernie, captain of the Robotics club."

"Ah, your new-found passion," he said.

Astrid did a double take. Could her dad see right into her soul? Then she realized he meant robotics.

"Yeah," she said. "I really like the club."

"That's great. It's nice to see you happy again. I've missed seeing you smile."

14 Back in Time

ASTRID TORE OPEN the letter from Waterloo.

We regret to inform you that your application was unsuccessful.

Did they not understand that she would die if she didn't get into the same school Bernie was going to? How else was she supposed to find out if Bernie liked her back? She had already decided that it would happen on a snowy Ontario day. They'd be at the library studying together, then they'd walk back to the dorms. They'd have dinner by candlelight in one of their rooms. When everything was just right, Astrid would tell Bernie how she felt. That there'd been something special between them from that first day in Robotics club.

And now Waterloo had gone and ruined the plan.

Despite her disappointment, Astrid hauled herself to Robotics. It was the only place in the world she could stand to be. Even if now she stood next to no chance with Bernie. Astrid knew she wasn't ready to say anything just yet. And there was no way Bernie would be ready to hear it.

Another blow was that Karsyn was back. Astrid took a deep breath and decided she'd take the high road by ignoring him. *He and Ivy should keep their business to themselves*, she thought.

Bernie gave everyone an assignment. Bernie and Karsyn were to work together on some code. Astrid had to make the levers that the robot would use to hold the boxes. Kind of like arms, but not. As she was gearing up, she thought it was kind of cool to have found a place on the crew. She'd come into this thing afraid that she would have nothing to contribute. And now cutting metal was her thing. When the goggles were in place and the ear protection was on, Astrid turned on the machine. Ranj was spotting her, doing a decent job of helping her guide the sheet into the machine.

The incision went well. She was pleased with the shape they made. It wouldn't be too hard to file. Then she measured it.

Uh-oh.

One-eighth of an inch too small. Too small was the worst thing. Too big, and you could sand it to fit. Too small, and you'd wasted really expensive material and a whole bunch of time.

Astrid couldn't face her team to tell them. Having to face Bernie.

"We have a screw up," Ranj said in a really loud voice.

Bernie and Aliyah came rushing over. "What happened?"

"It's too small." Astrid couldn't meet their eyes.

"We had just those two pieces of sheet metal," Bernie said.

"You didn't measure it first?" Aliyah asked.

The weight of their disappointment crashed down on top of the bad thoughts Astrid had been having all day. She could feel the tears coming. But she would not let Karsyn see her cry. No way. She sniffled. "I'm sorry I ruined it. I need some air."

Astrid bolted. Didn't even stop for her umbrella. There was no time. The tears were coming. Everything felt like a mistake now. What was the point of being part of a team if she was going to be the weak link? The one that let everyone down? What was the point of working hard if she wasn't going to have a future anyway? She thought about the Waterloo letter again. *Unsuccessful.*

Everyone in the club would go on to have their fabulous lives. But she'd still be weighing cups of yogourt and trying to master the art of smiling while dying inside so she could get more tips. Ugh. Why bother with any of it?

The rain hit her and she didn't care. She might as well look like a sewer rat. She felt like one.

"Hey! Wait up!"

Astrid turned. It was Bernie. Bernie had followed her outside the building and along the brick trail.

"I'm sorry I messed up, Bernie," Astrid said. "I'll pay for it. Where do you get sheet metal?"

"I didn't come out here to talk about the robot," Bernie said. "I wanted to make sure you were okay."

"That's not a very robot thing to do."

"What can I say? I am surprising myself right now."

"Can we walk for a bit?" Astrid asked. "I can't go back right away."

"Is it the robot part?"

"Of course it's the part. I feel bad about it. What if this puts us behind?"

"Aliyah has more metal somewhere."

"It's not just that. I'm out of my league here. I don't even know why I'm in this club. I'm just going to work in yogourt retail for the rest of my life anyway."

"Where's this coming from?"

"I got rejected from Waterloo."

"So? There are other schools."

"I'm seriously doubting whether I should bother. It's so expensive. I can't imagine coming out with that much debt."

"But you're young. You can pay it off."

"Only if I'm any good. What if I stink at my job the way I stink at being in this club?"

"You're off by an eighth of an inch and now you're some kind of failure for life? I don't get you. Why are you so hard on yourself?"

Astrid shrugged.

"What would Karsyn have done in the same situation?"

The question surprised her. "Uh . . . Asked for another piece of metal?"

"Exactly. That's all you need to do."

Astrid's eyes were strained from holding back the tears. And now she felt like she had been a drama queen. Bernie was right. It wasn't worth getting that upset about.

On impulse, she asked, "Can I have a hug?"

Bernie smiled in a crooked way that made her look puzzled. She put her arms around Astrid. It was awkward and sweet. Astrid could tell that Bernie was not much of a hugger. Neither was she, really. But the situation called for it. And it lasted a bit longer than she was expecting. Up close, Bernie smelled like laundry detergent.

"Let's get back," Bernie said as she pulled back.

Astrid knew Bernie was itching to go. It was a shocker that she'd left the club for a feelings-related issue to begin with.

As they headed back inside, Bernie slid her arm inside Astrid's, forming a loop. They walked in perfect stride with each other.

"This feels nice," Astrid said. "If I didn't know any better, I'd think you were trying to put the moves on me," she joked.

Bernie got quiet. Astrid looked over at her, but Bernie wouldn't meet her eyes. They walked back in silence. Now the looped arms seemed awkward. Astrid wished she hadn't made a joke of it, especially if it was going to change things. She had been enjoying it. Loving it. If she'd kept her mouth shut, maybe there'd be more of this in the future. Now she was sure she'd just gone and made it weird.

Aliyah had already found another piece of sheet metal. This time, Astrid would make the cut a hair too large and then sand it down. Maybe she wasn't going to Waterloo, but she wasn't going to leave Robotics either.

By the time Robotics was over, Astrid noticed that Bernie had not said a word all night. There had been no pressure to build anything. Even when Astrid had announced that her new cuts had come out perfectly, Bernie had been quiet.

"See you Thursday?" Astrid said on the way out.

Bernie looked up from the computer. "Yep."

"Are you going to stay here much longer?" Astrid asked. It was typical for Bernie to linger and close the place down. She often left with Aliyah, way after everyone else had gone home.

"There's a snag in the code."

"Okay," Astrid said. She knew she couldn't offer to help. "Thursday, then."

"Yep."

Astrid walked to the bus stop feeling like she'd messed things up. And not just the cut. Bernie had come after her to make sure she was okay. *Why did I have to make it awkward by joking?* Astrid asked herself. *Why couldn't I just enjoy the moment?*

Bernie had never even hinted she might be queer. Was she? Wasn't she? Maybe it wasn't her style to put labels on things. After all, this was someone who identified as a robot.

15 Sabotage

ASTRID'S WEEK had been killer. Working late and worrying about everything was getting her down. She overheard her parents talking about the whole lot of them moving in with her grandparents in Saskatoon. Their apartment's paper-thin walls were a real security risk for sensitive information. She also heard talk about how they needed to stay here to let her and her brother finish school where they started. The argument was that they'd already had too much disruption with the move and the new frugal living. She didn't know if her brother listened in on these conversations the way she did. She didn't ask him. He was wearing headphones. She hoped he was listening to something and not just blocking them all out.

School wasn't going much better. In Math, she knew she bombed the last question on her test. Her brain had been mush after working and there had been no time to go back to the textbook. She hadn't managed to study before the shift. She hadn't slept well before the test. She wouldn't get her mark for a while, but everything counted. Every wrong answer was one step closer to a destiny that involved wearing an apron.

Unable to afford the time even to commute, Astrid buried her head in her Math textbook all the way out to UBC. She felt self-conscious about the university students looking at her Grade Twelve book. When she walked into Robotics club, nothing had changed since she was last there. Bernie was still huddled at the computer, wearing the exact same outfit. Presumably, in the three days that had passed, she'd gone home and done laundry. But it was still weird to see her crouched over like that, completely tuned out from the rest of the world.

"Bernie?" Astrid asked.

Aliyah jumped in. "She's fixated. It's been like this for a while now." Aliyah sounded like a nurse taking care of a patient.

Astrid went and waved her hand in front of Bernie's face.

Bernie flinched. "Oh. What?"

"Nothing. Hello."

"It's messed. And I can't tell why. I know I did everything right. But it's just not working."

"Walk me through it," Astrid said. Sure, coding was out of her comfort zone for now. But she'd get there eventually. Maybe a fresh pair of eyes would help.

"I don't even know what I'm looking for. How would *you* know?"

Astrid shrugged. "Just an offer."

"I'm sorry. Thank you. I'm just frustrated."

"Well, yeah. It's been a long time you've been at this. Has anyone else seen it?"

"Karsyn. I sent it to him last night. He's good at this, so I figured I'd run it by him."

Astrid got a sinking feeling. "Was it working before you sent it to him?"

"I thought it was. It seemed to be."

"Do you think he messed with it?"

"Why would he do that? We're on the same team."

"Yes, but he's on two teams. And, I dunno, this isn't an allegation. But don't you think he'd get a kick out of seeing you like this?"

Before Bernie could respond, Karsyn arrived. "Well, well, well," he said. "What do we have here? Not an operational box lifter yet, that's for sure."

"I'm stuck," Bernie admitted. "You said last night this all looked solid. So help me figure out why it's not working."

"Let's see now," he said. "Scoot over."

Bernie moved aside to let Karsyn sit in front of the computer.

"Here's the problem," he announced. "A missing semicolon. No big deal. Rookie mistake."

"That can't be it," Bernie said. "I know that was there. I double checked it before I sent it to you. I've made that mistake in the past."

Astrid looked at Aliyah. Aliyah looked surprised and arched an eyebrow.

"Happens to everyone," Karsyn said.

"I'm positive, though." Bernie whipped out her iPhone and scrolled through some pictures. She clicked on one to enlarge it and held it up in front of everyone. "See? It's correct here."

"You take photos of your own code?" Karsyn asked.

"I document everything."

"Sounds kind of paranoid to me," he said with a hint of a laugh. It was like he was making fun of Bernie.

Aliyah and Astrid made eye contact again. This was not good.

"I like to keep track of every step of the way,"

Bernie said. "I also back up my files. I'm not a moron."

Aliyah blurted out, "Karsyn, did you tamper with Bernie's code?"

"We're on the same team. Why would I do that?" He looked on the verge of outrage. But Astrid could sense something desperate and fake about it.

"Maybe so you could waltz in here and fix it like you just did?" Astrid ventured.

"Karsyn, let's talk outside," Aliyah said.

"I didn't do anything," Karsyn protested. "I was just messing around."

"So you did mess around with Bernie's code?" Astrid asked.

"It was just to be funny."

"What's funny about stressing me out?" Bernie asked. "Can't you tell I'm already a basket case?"

"You need to lighten up, Bernie," said Karsyn with a smug smile. "I've always said that about you. You have to learn how to take a joke and roll with things. All these years, you've always been so serious about everything."

"That's how I am," Bernie said. "I can't change that."

"If you're going to be a leader, you have to know how to act like one. You can't go and get all defensive about every little thing." Karsyn said.

"We're stepping out, Karsyn," Aliyah said. "Let's go."

16 Rivalry

"I'M SORRY," Astrid said when she was finally alone with Bernie. "It really sucks that he put you through that."

"I should have known," said Bernie, shaking her head. "It's been pranks like that since eighth grade. When will I learn?"

"It's not your fault for trusting a teammate. You have to be able to rely on your team."

"Maybe I do need to lighten up. There are more

important things than code. I've been sitting here for hours."

"That's because you care."

"Maybe too much."

"Don't question yourself. This isn't about you." Astrid put her hand on Bernie's arm. Bernie, still sitting, pulled Astrid in for a hug.

"Thanks."

Aliyah came back without Karsyn. She looked troubled as she explained to them. "I've had the privilege of running this kind of club, here and in Toronto, for many years. I've never kicked anybody out until today."

Astrid tried to determine what Bernie was feeling. Shock, maybe. Bernie sat there staring, like the last ten minutes had short circuited her wiring.

"You know, my mom was in engineering," Aliyah said. "But that was a different time. She was the first woman in my family to go to university. And the fact that she went into engineering — well, I marvel at it. Getting through school was hard. She thought it would get easier on the job, but nope. When she got pregnant with me, she gave it all up."

"Whoa," Astrid said.

"Did she want you to go into engineering?" Bernie asked.

"She wanted me to choose my own path," said Aliyah. "But she taught me so much. Some kids play with cars and train sets. My mom and I used to build them from scratch. I guess you could say she encouraged me."

"And she never went back to work after that?" Astrid asked. She felt like the question was too personal as soon as it left her mouth. But she felt she really needed to know.

"No, she never did. My parents moved to Canada. She would have had to start all over to graduate with credentials from a program here. I guess she just couldn't face it. But she still builds things."

"Wow," Astrid said. "Very cool."

"I guess that's why I'm interested in mentoring future engineers. It's one thing to help my students. But it's a whole other thing to encourage the next generation. The ones who are just getting a start."

"I still don't know if I'm going into engineering," Astrid said.

"You don't have to decide yet."

"I don't feel like I have the foundation. I can't code worth crap."

"You can learn. Nobody comes to this knowing everything already. I didn't. Even Bernie didn't." Aliyah turned to the team captain. "Right, Bernie?"

Bernie spoke to Astrid. "I don't feel like I have what it takes either. I guess that's why I'm so serious about getting this thing to work. If I can do that, maybe I can convince myself I'm okay at this."

"Bernie, you're better than okay at this," Astrid said.

Bernie shrugged. Astrid could see how hard it was for her to talk about herself. "What's going to happen with Karsyn now?" Bernie asked.

Aliyah said, "He still has his school team. He'll be fine."

"Guys like him will always be fine," Astrid said. Maybe it was rubbing salt in the wound. But he wasn't here to hear, and she wasn't going to miss him.

"I feel bad," Bernie said. "Maybe he really was just joking around."

"To be honest," said Aliyah. "This wasn't the first time I considered letting him go. It's been a pattern of behaviour."

"Karsyn stood up for me many times over the years," said Bernie. "I don't know. Sometimes I think he is one of the closest friends I ever had because he helped me a lot."

"And also sabotaged you," Astrid added.

"I get it," Aliyah said. "It's complicated. I had a rival, too. A couple, actually. It's a weird thing. You can appreciate everything about a person who helps you move forward. Even if they do it by making you stand your ground and hold them at a distance."

"I guess he can't be all bad," Astrid admitted.

"I mean, Ivy obviously sees something in him. Something I admit I'm failing to see."

"Ivy?" Aliyah asked.

"My ex-girlfriend. She's going out with him." Astrid was surprised that saying it didn't hurt more.

"No wonder you hate him," Aliyah said, nodding. "I was curious what that was all about."

Astrid rolled her eyes. "Many things. I also don't enjoy him and his friends hounding me every Sunday when they come for frozen yogourt. But enough about my hate-on."

As if she had one mystery solved, Aliyah turned to Bernie. "Bernie, it's okay to have mixed feelings. And I'm sorry that I'm taking away the one other person in this group who's good at coding. But I stand by it. I want a team that can work together. That involves not setting people up for failure."

At Bernie's stricken look, Astrid chimed in. "I might not be able to find an out-of-place semicolon for you. But I'll build and cut and drill whatever you need."

17 Tangled Code

FOR ASTRID, Robotics got a lot easier without Karsyn there. Balancing work and school and the club suddenly didn't seem as hard. *Must be the team dynamic,* she thought. She didn't spend every trip on the 99 dreading a complex social interaction. Miraculously, Karsyn and his friends stopped coming in for yogourt, too. Maybe the mighty dictatorship had been toppled. The king was dead.

Inspired, Astrid brought a box of chocolates to

Robotics. She was happy to celebrate. She figured everyone else would be, too. But she walked in on Ranj hovering around Bernie. A closer look revealed that Bernie had been crying.

"I can't do it. I don't know how." Bernie sniffled.

Astrid picked up a blue workshop towel and passed it to her. No tissues in sight.

Bernie took it and rubbed it under her nose. "We're doomed," she pronounced. "It's not working."

"Can't Aliyah help us?" asked Astrid.

"She's not allowed to. Any interference by anyone who's not in high school is an automatic disqualification."

"But this directive is obviously a first-year university formula," said Azi. "Even second-year."

"Whether that's true or not, I can't do it," Bernie said.

"I know what I'm talking about," said Azi. "My brother is in second year. I've seen him do stuff like this."

"Does your brother want to join our group?" Astrid asked.

"Why don't you just call the judges and tell them we have help from NASA?" Ranj said.

It bothered Astrid that the group actually seemed to need Karsyn. Her muscles were tense. She could feel it in her skin whenever she thought about Karsyn being back on the team. Still, she found herself questioning if maybe she shouldn't have put up such a stink about him. If she hadn't made a point about him being a dick, Bernie and Aliyah might have forgiven the coding "joke." Aliyah might not have kicked him off the team. This was her fault.

But what could she do? *You can't just learn this stuff overnight*, she thought. Real life wasn't like the movies where a character could go through a studying montage and suddenly be full of knowledge.

"I'm sorry," Astrid said.

"For what?" Bernie asked.

"I feel that, without me, we'd still have Karsyn."

"Quit making things about you, Astrid," Azi said. "We have a *real* problem."

"We have to hit the books," Bernie said. "I see

no other way. We all just have to read every textbook we have in this room. And all the blueprints to every robot on every open software site across the globe. This is about willpower and hard work. Who's in?"

Everyone was.

They spread out around the workshop. Bernie and Ranj had their laptops and did their reading from a screen. Astrid sat with a massive clunker of a textbook spread out on the band saw. There were pages and pages with lines and squiggles that made no sense to her at all. She didn't even know what she was looking for.

Astrid was lost in the text when Bernie got up from her desk and came over. "I just want to say thanks. You stuck with this. With me. And it means a lot."

"Where would I go?" Astrid asked. It surprised her that Bernie could think about anything emotional at a time like this.

"I dunno."

"I don't think I can learn coding by osmosis in the next two hours. But I can probably work on our transportation plan instead." It had been on Astrid's mind that they'd have to get the whole team plus the robot to a school near the border to showcase it. They'd have to take apart the robot and put it together on the day of the competition. Sometimes she'd wake up in the middle of the night from a nightmare that their project would arrive like a brand new Lego set, all in pieces.

"That'd be great," Bernie said.

"I'll see what I can do."

Just then Astrid's phone rang. Ivy's face came up. Astrid said, "I should take this."

"Of course."

Astrid took the call as she walked outside. It was easy to hear that Ivy was upset. "You were right about him," Ivy said, her voice soft and sad.

"I'm sorry," Astrid said. "What happened?"

"I left him. He needed me to be someone I'm not. He wanted me to tell him I would only be interested in him forever. And that I'd never be in another queer relationship."

Astrid stood in the rain and listened. As Ivy's story

unfolded, Astrid felt like the world was shifting back into some sort of order. She hadn't been wrong about Karsyn. She had been right about what she and Ivy used to have. Her jealousy and hurt melted, and she finally felt like she was talking with a friend. The edge that had been between them ever since they broke up was gone. Guards down. No pretending that everything was fabulous and Instagrammable.

"I'm really happy for you," Astrid said. "I know that might sound weird for a breakup. But when you leave someone not worthy of you, I think it's cause for celebration."

Astrid got Ivy to talk. For the next thirty minutes, Ivy dished about everything and how it all went sideways. They got off the phone with a promise to meet up soon. Not to talk about Karsyn. Just to spend some time together as friends. Astrid's mind was at peace for the first time in a long time. She could feel the smile on her face as she entered the workshop. Maybe working out the ins and outs of the human heart would even improve her ability to understand code.

"You're not going to believe what happened," she said to Bernie. "Ivy kicked Karsyn to the curb. She really let him have it."

Bernie stared back blankly.

"Well? Isn't that great?" asked Astrid.

"Yeah, yeah. Good for her. I need to solve this problem."

"I'm sorry I shared. Maybe I thought you'd share my joy."

"Good for *you* then," Bernie said as she turned back to her screen.

Astrid felt like a door had been slammed in her face. She didn't know what she'd said or done.

Bernie let out a breath. It was the ultimate signal for Astrid to go away. But for some reason, she just stood there.

Without looking at Astrid, Bernie spoke. "I really do think it's best if you worked on transportation for now. From home if you can."

"Oh. Um. So I should just leave?"

"You said it yourself. You're not going to be able to help with this."

"All right."

"It's not that late," Bernie looked at her watch. "You can probably still catch up with Ivy."

"I just did catch up with Ivy. That's what that whole update was about." Astrid made a face. Where did her connection with Bernie go sideways? Why was Bernie giving her such attitude? Maybe she didn't have those ins and outs worked out after all.

18 Decoding Feelings

ASTRID PACKED UP her stuff and was about to head out. But then she stopped. It felt too weird, like she was being punished. She knew that Bernie saw her in the wrong. But she had no idea what crime she'd committed.

"Bernie, will you walk me to the bus stop?" Astrid asked.

Bernie stared at her for a moment without saying anything. Astrid didn't know how to bear the cold silence. Finally Bernie spoke so softly that Astrid had to lean close to hear. "Are you sure you want me to?"

"Um . . . I'm asking, right?" Astrid said. "Why are you being weird?"

"I'm not being weird," Bernie whispered. "I have a ton of stuff to do."

"It'll take ten minutes."

"Okay."

Bernie followed Astrid outside. Once they were out in the rain, Astrid put up her umbrella and held it between them. "You want to share?"

Bernie stayed back outside the circle of the umbrella. Astrid created a loop with her arm hoping they could walk together like last time. Bernie walked alongside her, under the umbrella but with a terrible distance between them.

"What's going on with us?" Astrid asked.

"*Us?*" Bernie asked.

"Yeah. Ever since I came back inside from the phone call. Are you mad that I was happy to hear about Karsyn's butt getting kicked to the curb?" Astrid asked. "I know I can be a horrible human being."

"No, Karsyn's not my friend. He's not my enemy either. I have no feelings."

"Well, obviously you do have feelings. You're mad at me. Or something."

They walked to the bus loop in silence. Astrid tried to make sense of Bernie, but she couldn't. She missed the way it was all the times things were easy between them. She missed being at Bernie's house, in her room. She missed the easy way they had laughed together at the conference.

They stood together quietly under Astrid's umbrella, keeping as much distance as two people under one umbrella could keep. There were at least fifty other students standing around in clusters getting rained on.

With no words to try, Astrid stared at the idle bus off to the side of the loop. Finally the bus driver went inside and turned on the sign that said *99 Commercial-Broadway*. Then he sat down. Astrid felt like the slowness of all of this would kill her.

The bus pulled up in front of the crowd. The students piled on. Astrid was about to go.

"Wait," Bernie said.

Astrid turned back to her. "Okay."

As the bus drove off, Bernie blurted out, "So are you getting back together with Ivy?"

"Oh, God, no." Astrid said, horrified. "Wait a second. Why would you even think that?" *So that's what this was really about*, she thought. The idea that Bernie might be jealous thrilled her.

"You were so happy when you came back from the call."

"I was happy because I'm a horrible person who wants to see Karsyn suffer. And it was so good, the way Ivy gave it to him."

"Your face actually lights up when you talk about her."

"What?" Astrid didn't believe it. "No, my face lights up in a sadistic way when I see karma unfold."

"So you're not still in love with her?"

"No." She shook her head. "Where's that coming

from?" *Hasn't my attraction to Bernie been super friggin' obvious?* Astrid asked herself. She thought the whole club could tell.

Bernie shrugged.

"That relationship feels like a lifetime ago. I was a different person." Astrid took a step closer to Bernie.

"How?"

"Ivy wanted what most people our age want. Good times, fun summers, great photos to put on Instagram. I lost all interest and ability in that practically overnight."

"Is that why she dumped you?"

"Pretty much. I couldn't go to that music festival. I mean, I could have. I did have the money saved. My parents told me to go enjoy myself anyway. But I couldn't do it."

"And she was upset about that?" Bernie looked surprised and empathetic.

"Well, she'd been looking forward to it for, like, a year. She told me I abandoned her. She's got a flair for drama."

"Oh." It was easy to see that Bernie wasn't impressed.

"Yeah, it all sounds so immature now. I'm not sure you would have liked me very much back then. To be honest, I'm kind of glad things have been harder for me this past year. It's made me see things I didn't used to see."

"Like what?"

"Like how much it matters to have goals and work hard."

"Really?"

"Totally. I mean, look at you. You're set up. You have a cool future ahead. That's got to feel really good."

"I don't know if it's cool. I've just always wanted to go to Waterloo."

"Your focus is cool."

"You think?"

"One hundred percent."

"No one has ever called me cool before." Bernie said.

Another bus pulled up. Astrid's belly felt like a helium balloon, pulling her up toward the sky. She didn't want this to end. She wondered if maybe she should ask Bernie to go somewhere where they could talk. But she knew Bernie wanted to get back to the club.

Bernie grabbed hold of a strap on Astrid's backpack and let her finger dangle on it. To Astrid it was almost as if they were holding hands. It was like there was some kind of electric charge in that gesture that went all the way through her body. Mostly, she was surprised that Bernie was so forward. Of course, it could mean nothing. Maybe all of it was in Astrid's head. The chemistry, the connection. Everything.

"See you next time," Astrid said as she got on the bus.

"Text me later if you want," Bernie said.

"Okay, I will." Astrid went to take a seat at the back. It was crammed and she could no longer see Bernie through the crowd. She looked out the window and tried not to smile, but she could feel in her cheeks that she was grinning. Staring out the window of the bus, her heart pounded.

I'm in love, she thought.

With someone who is moving across the country.

19 It's Alive

ASTRID'S PHONE BUZZED loudly in her bag. She was not supposed to check it at work. But the yogourt shop was quiet. She was fifteen minutes from closing the doors. She grabbed the phone. Bernie's face flashed at her.

"Hey," Astrid said. She realized it was the first time they were speaking on the phone. Always texts with Bernie the robot.

"It's working!" Bernie yelled. Her voice was ecstatic. "It's moving around right now!"

"Oh my God."

"You have to come."

"I'm just finishing up my shift."

"I'll come get you."

Astrid grabbed a large container and made a big swirly tub of every flavour and every topping and sauce in the place. The ultimate. She crammed it into the freezer in the back. For the next fifteen minutes, she wiped down all the surfaces with bleach. She covered all the toppings and cleaned the dishes. She churned the day's receipts out of the till for the owner to see the next morning.

It had been a slow night for tips, but that hardly mattered. Astrid had never been more excited. She took her apron off at ten o'clock on the dot and tossed it in the laundry hamper. She flung on her denim jacket. She grabbed her canvas bag and the big tub from the freezer, along with two spoons wrapped in plastic.

Outside, Bernie was already waiting in her parents' SUV. Astrid opened the passenger side. Bernie was glistening with excitement.

"You're not going to believe it." Bernie had never sounded so excited. "I mean, you will. You know what it's supposed to look like. But it's just so different when it all comes together. When it works."

Bernie is beaming, thought Astrid. *Cutest sight ever.* "When did it happen?" she asked.

"Literally just an hour ago. We were going to wait for you, but . . ."

"Are Azi and Ranj still there?"

"I don't think so. Maybe. I told them to just lock up if they leave. Aliyah left earlier."

Astrid couldn't help but feel special. There was no way Bernie would have left her pride and joy. Not unless she wanted Astrid to be there so badly that she was willing to chance letting others lock up. That was huge.

They parked illegally right behind the Robotics club.

"What if you get a ticket?" Astrid asked.

"You have to see this. It can't wait. Let's go." Bernie was practically vibrating.

They ran from the car like they were in an action movie.

The building was dark. The door to the Robotics club was locked. Bernie turned the key and flicked on the lights.

There, in the middle of their workshop space, a big, beautiful structure stood tall. Bernie went toward it. She picked up the remote that was left lying on the table.

"Watch," Bernie said.

She clicked a few buttons. The robot turned on and moved over to some boxes at the side of the room. First it scooped one box up with the prongs. It reminded Astrid of a papa penguin protecting its egg by pulling it under the skin folds of its belly. When the first box was hoisted up, the robot approached another box. The first box went up on the lever and the second box got pulled up onto the platform. Again. Again. Again. Now there were five boxes stacked. The robot went for one more. Just like that, it was holding six boxes.

"Six boxes!" Bernie squealed. She was clapping her hands together.

"Oh my God." Astrid was in awe of what they had made.

"I'm so proud of our design."

"It's like we have an alien love child."

Bernie laughed. "Let's call him Robbie."

"Awwwww. Robbie!"

Astrid placed the yogourt treat on the floor in between them. "We have to celebrate."

Astrid could see Bernie was torn between leaving the machine alone or taking a second to sit back and enjoy it all. Astrid presented the yogourt. They ate and watched the robot stack boxes again like it was the best show in town. Because it was.

It had already been late when they arrived and soon it would be midnight.

"I'll drive you home, Astrid," Bernie said.

Astrid didn't know if she was ready for that. But she sure would prefer it to getting on the 99. Her muscles ached from the length of the day. First school, then work and then a late-night robot demo that made her feel like she'd never sleep again.

"I'm so wired," Bernie said.

"Me too," Astrid agreed. They walked back to the SUV. No ticket. Astrid felt like the universe was on their side for the night. "Did you want to go home right away?"

"Why? What did you have in mind?" Bernie asked as they climbed in.

Astrid shrugged. "Take me somewhere."

"Like where?"

"I dunno. The lake?"

Bernie left the illegal parking space and turned left at the next light. Before long, they were on a bench looking out at Trout Lake.

"I can't believe we did it." Bernie was still over the moon.

"Mostly *you* did it," Astrid pointed out.

"You helped."

Astrid looked over to see Bernie staring straight ahead at the quiet evening ripples. "I'm really glad I got to be a part of that," Astrid said softly. "Best part of this year, actually."

"Really?" Bernie looked over at her.

"Hundred percent."

Bernie leaned forward with her eyes closed. *What now?* Astrid wondered. *Does this mean she wants to kiss?* Astrid would never just go for it without knowing. So she touched Bernie's face. Bernie opened her eyes. Astrid could see that she had been pouting her lips. Mostly because she stopped doing that once she saw Astrid looking at her. Astrid caressed Bernie's cheek with the back of her hand.

"I like that," Bernie said.

"Me, too," Astrid said. "So should we skinny dip?" She was half joking, but only half. It was that kind of magical evening.

"Now?"

"Why not?"

"I guess because I was enjoying being right here with you." Bernie reached out and grabbed Astrid's hand to move it back up to her cheek.

"You like it when I touch your cheek?" Astrid longed to hear Bernie admit it.

Bernie nodded. She leaned in close again. "It makes me want to kiss you," she said.

This time, Astrid was the one who closed her eyes. Their bodies were close together but barely touching. The magnetic pull between them made Astrid dizzy.

The kiss was warm and sweet. And it lasted for a long time. When they pulled back, Astrid knew that things had changed forever. The unspoken uncertainty between them had been acted upon. They had altered the course of history. No way they could pretend like it hadn't happened. Like they were just friends, or just robot enthusiasts with a shared project.

"I really like you," Astrid said. "I've loved spending all this time with you." She wanted to tell Bernie she loved her, but maybe that was too big of a word for now. Too scary, even if it was the truth.

"I really like you, too," Bernie said. She looked down, and Astrid could see a shyness steal over her. "I'm surprised I was able to say that."

"You can tell me anything you want to."

"I've never told anyone I like them before. I've never liked anyone the way I like you."

They kissed some more.

Before long it was four a.m.

"My parents are going to freak," Bernie said. "I've never been out this late. A lot of firsts in one night."

Back in the SUV, Bernie turned the key in the ignition as Astrid buckled up. There was already a hint of daylight coming through the darkness.

"I'm going to be such a zombie at school," Astrid said. "But whatever. Wouldn't trade this night for anything."

Bernie kept her eyes on the road. But she smiled.

20 Take a Chance

THEY PULLED UP outside of Astrid's home and shared
one last kiss. Then Astrid went around the back of the
house and down into her family's basement suite. She
turned the key slowly and quietly. She tiptoed to her
room and plunked herself down on the mattress next
to her sleeping brother.

When her alarm went off at 6:30, she was still
fully dressed. Jolted out of her sleep, she felt suddenly
warm all over. In her mind, she savoured everything

that happened. She sat up and turned off her alarm.

There, in the cold light of the morning, was a text from Bernie. It said, I can't do this.

Astrid's mind went totally blank except for one thought: What?

She flopped back down onto the bed. The text had come in about ten minutes after Astrid got home. Bernie must have driven back to her place and realized what a terrible thing it would be to be with her. Astrid pulled the blanket up over her head. School be damned. She wasn't going anywhere. Her heart filled with a combination of guilt, heartbreak and wondering if she'd pushed Bernie into doing something she didn't want to do. And also longing. She could still feel the warmth of Bernie's lips on hers.

"Get up, get up!" her brother shouted.

"I'm sick. Leave me alone," she said.

"I'm telling Mom."

"Go ahead. I haven't missed a single day of school this year. I'm staying home today."

Her brother shut the door behind him when he left.

Finally she was alone. She cried. She could hear the footsteps of the family upstairs. It felt like they were walking all over her crushed dreams. If Bernie rejected her, what was the point of even going to the Robotics championships? This was their thing together. Unless she had completely misunderstood.

She texted Bernie. Can we at least talk?

Bernie's reply started right away. Astrid watched in suspense, waiting to see Bernie's response. But then the dots indicating the typing went away.

Astrid pulled the curtains closed and changed into her real PJs. There was no point to being awake.

She napped until two o'clock. Normally she'd be in Math by then, but nothing mattered.

Bernie had texted back while Astrid slept. I can meet you after school.

She wrote back, I skipped today. I'm at home. Come over?

There in fifteen, Bernie wrote back.

Astrid was sitting on the curb. She didn't want Bernie ringing the doorbell to the landlord's place upstairs.

When Bernie got out of the SUV, it was obvious she'd been crying.

"You ditched out too?" Astrid asked. "Unthinkable for a non-feeling robot."

"I'm not non-feeling," Bernie said.

"You just don't have feelings for me," Astrid said. She sounded full of self-pity, even to herself.

"That's not true. I just . . . I can't. There's so many layers of *can't*."

Astrid sighed. "Start with the first one." She took Bernie's hand. She led her through the old wooden gate around to the back of the house and down the stairs. "No one's here until my brother comes home around three-thirty."

"Okay," Bernie said.

"Watch your head when you go through the door. I think this used to be a crawl space back when the house was built."

Bernie followed her inside. They sat on the

uncomfortable IKEA furniture. Sitting across from Bernie, Astrid felt like her insides were wrenched into a knot. Less than twelve hours ago, she'd been convinced this was true love. Now she was questioning everything.

"I have a list." Bernie said.

"It figures."

"One. We're moving apart. Two. I have to keep my focus. Three. I haven't been able to focus for the last few weeks because I have been thinking about you. Four. I've never kissed anyone before and I didn't think the first time would be with a girl."

"Are you disappointed?"

"No."

"Are you scared about it? I mean, coming out can be kinda intense."

"Yeah. Scared. Maybe a bit weirded out. Like how did *I* not know this about *myself?*"

Astrid nodded. She understood what Bernie meant, even if it hurt to hear the words. "It's okay to not know, you know, before you know."

"That's why I can't do this. I don't want you to be with someone who doesn't completely and totally know. This is pretty new information to me."

Even in matters of the heart, Bernie's analytical, Astrid thought. *What's the right thing to say to someone like that?*

"How new? When did you think differently about us? About yourself?"

"Um . . . Maybe at the lecture?"

"Really?" Astrid was strangely hopeful. That was longer ago than she had expected.

"Why?"

Astrid shrugged. "I didn't get that off of you that day."

"Well, when did you?"

"Mmmm. Maybe at the library?"

"Definitely at the library," Bernie said.

Is she blushing? Astrid sucked in her bottom lip thoughtfully. "Okay. I'm glad I wasn't wrong about that," she said, relieved.

Bernie smiled. "You weren't."

"So about that list. I know you're moving. I have

no clue what the heck I'll be up to next year. But that's months from now."

"You think it's better to fall in love and start the academic year heartbroken?"

"You think you'll fall in love?" Astrid's eyes widened. She couldn't help but smile.

Bernie shrugged. "I didn't say that."

"You kind of did."

"Okay, well maybe I kind of already have."

Astrid hugged Bernie. Then she burst into tears. She wasn't even sure why she was crying. Wasn't this a happy time? Hadn't she expected this talk to go far worse? But she was overcome with feelings.

She tried to explain. "I was so afraid you wouldn't want to see me anymore. I would have been crushed."

"Really?"

"Bernie, I don't know how to tell you, but you make this world make sense."

"Because I'm a cyborg?"

Astrid laughed. "Yeah, maybe."

Bernie took Astrid's hand and guided it to

her cheek. "I really liked it when you touched me like that."

Astrid watched Bernie's face soften to the point of looking squishy. "We can go really slow," she said. "We don't have to label it or even tell anyone. I don't care. I just want us to be okay."

"I don't mind people knowing," Bernie said. "I just . . . I don't know. It's all kind of a lot. We need to slay at the competition."

"We'll slay. We'll totally slay."

21 Round One

ON THE MORNING of the competition, Astrid woke up super early. It was so early she didn't dare make a smoothie for fear of waking up her family. She had some instant oatmeal and was out the door and on her bike by 6:30. She had to catch the school bus taking them to Seaquam Secondary School in Delta.

On the bus, it was just their group and Robbie. Astrid sat next to Bernie, who yawned.

Even her yawns are cute.

Astrid imagined waking up next to Bernie. But then she snuffed out the thought. This was The Big Day. They had to concentrate.

Get it together, Astrid. No cute crush thoughts. Only robots.

The gym was packed. This was not like the conference. It was much more intense. Upon arrival, Bernie and Astrid ran for a cart, dodging between the other buses parked in the back of the school. The sun was shining and it was breezy but warm. Azi, Ranj and Aliyah were all huddled around Robbie trying to finesse how best to move the machine out of the back of the bus.

Astrid had worked out that they move Robbie in four separate large pieces and assemble him on site. The problem was that he wasn't exactly light. His weight was good in theory and difficult in transportation. But Astrid was sure it would make the difference in the battle.

There was an announcement. Fifteen minutes to get the robots set up in the arena. That was barely enough time to get Robbie put together. And they didn't even know where they were going. This was the moment of truth. Adrenaline coursed through Astrid. She imagined Robbie blowing the competition out of the water.

As they got set up, Astrid took a glance around. The bleachers were filled with students from around the Lower Mainland. And some from as far away as Vancouver Island, Nelson and Prince George. Crazy.

Astrid kept a close watch on Bernie, who looked as if she was about to lose her mind. She had the clipboard with the checklist. She was even wearing a whistle and ballcap. She was in her element. Aliyah did her best to be a chill presence, but even she looked pretty high strung. Azi and Ranj were already sitting down. Astrid joined them.

On the hard wood seating, waiting for one of those adults huddled over in the corner to announce the start of the day, Astrid spotted Karsyn. He was off in the distance but easy to see. His team was all wearing their private school uniforms. *Weird choice*, Astrid thought. They stuck out against the rest of the assembly. Maybe they thought they were better than everyone else.

Astrid watched Karsyn. He seemed calm and collected. She tried looking at him through the eyes of a younger Bernie. Or of Ivy. He wasn't bad looking. He had confidence and good hair. But try as she might, Astrid could not imagine what it would be like to have a crush on him. And it wasn't just that he was a boy. It was like he was all surface, with no insides to want to get to know better.

Aliyah and Bernie joined the group. Bernie passed Astrid a cup of coffee. Not that she needed it, but Astrid took a sip. It was just right. As Astrid sat there surrounded by her team, still peering at Karsyn, she realized that he reminded her of the person she used to be. There was a time when she would have come across with that kind of confidence, too. Or that kind of shallowness.

The MC introduced each team. When it was their turn, they had to stand up and wave their hands in the air. Theirs was the smallest of all the teams gathered. Just one tiny little club, courtesy of the best mentor ever. When they said Aliyah's name, all four of them cheered so loud they drowned out the rest of the applause. Astrid thought about how amazing it was that Aliyah had given up her social life for them. Had really taken an interest in all of them. Aliyah had become majorly important to her in such a short time.

Suspended from the ceiling was a massive net containing seventy-five or maybe one hundred cardboard boxes. When the airhorn went off, the net was released and all the boxes tumbled to the ground. Now it was up to them to steer Robbie from way up where they were sitting. Bernie was holding on to the controller like she was playing the most intense video game of her life. The gym was nothing but yelling and screaming. It was almost impossible to follow what was happening. So much activity. Some robots fell over. A couple of kids tried to jump the barrier and got disqualified. Robbie only had two boxes. They seemed harder to stack here than in the workshop. Was it the size? Were they heavier than the test boxes? Or was there just too much chaos all around?

Each time Robbie got near a box, the box shuffled

away along the floor and not into Robbie's grasp. Astrid peeked over at Karsyn's team's robot. It had big long arms just like his original idea. They had a big hoop to catch the boxes and had managed to collect at least twice as many boxes as any other team.

The alarm sounded. That was the end of Round One. Astrid looked at her team. They were tense. It was obvious they hadn't won, or even placed, in the first round. Even though they had agreed not to distract each other, Astrid really wanted to put her arms around Bernie. Bernie had said for the good of the team, they shouldn't say or show anything about their being together until after the battle, so she didn't. But watching Bernie's disappointment was hard on Astrid.

There was a half-hour break. All the teams regrouped with their robots. The boxes were hoisted up again. The MC declared Karsyn's team the winner of the first round. Astrid looked over to find the members of his team hardly surprised. They might as well have been filing their nails while everyone else was biting theirs.

♥ ♥ ♥

When the MC announced the beginning of Round Two, Astrid couldn't find Bernie. She ran outside to find Bernie pacing back and forth. She looked like a smoker who didn't smoke.

This time Astrid did put her arms around Bernie. But Bernie was stiff. She stood still, arms at her sides, looking like she was about to cry.

"It's not over," Astrid said.

"I just don't get why it worked so much better at the workshop than here. Robbie couldn't seem to get a grip. On the boxes, I mean."

"What if you lined up Robbie to take boxes that are cornered against the sides of the arena? Push the boxes there if you have to."

"Maybe," Bernie said. "The gym floor is more slippery than the cement floor we've been practising on."

"Yep. You'll have to create the proper resistance."

"Let's get back in."

"Yep."

22 Finding Your Feet

AN AIRHORN started Round Two and the gym went nuts again. Astrid had not heard so much yelling and screaming in her life. Bernie stayed cool under pressure. There Robbie was, far away from the other action, sticking to the sides of the arena. One box. Two boxes. Three boxes. It was working.

"Only two more minutes!" yelled Azi.

"Keep going!" Ranj exclaimed.

Bernie maneuvered Robbie along the walls, using the support to close in on the boxes. They were up to four now. Box five was just a few feet away. He got it. Six was over on the side. Would he make it in time? Robbie was not a fast robot. But slow and steady worked. Bernie got Robbie over there and picked up the sixth box just seconds before the buzzer.

At the end of this round, everyone hugged everyone. This time Astrid was too intent to pay attention to Karsyn's team. Now she could see they had picked up five boxes. That meant her own team did better. That meant they won the round. Bernie let out a big cheer. Astrid watched as the tension melted from her.

It was time for a few words from the sponsors, and then lunch. During the break, Astrid and Bernie went around to look at the robots.

"There's something too sophisticated about this," Bernie said as they examined the robot built by Karsyn's team. "Remember how he said he didn't know how to do the math and coding for it?" Bernie was clearly suspicious.

For once Astrid didn't want to say anything. She was happy they had won the second round. She was hopeful they could win the third. That was all that mattered to her. But Bernie left her and approached Aliyah.

Astrid watched as Bernie said something to Aliyah. Aliyah looked toward where Astrid was standing next to what Astrid couldn't help but think of as Karsyn's robot. Aliyah gave Bernie a serious look and pointed toward the MC. Bernie went to him next. By the time Bernie got back, there were only fifteen minutes left of lunch. It was impossible to think about eating. But they did go outside, open their brown bags and drink their juice boxes.

"I've never been a rat before in my life," Bernie said. "But it's no secret that he has tutors up the wazoo. And that's okay. But not when they secretly interfere in a competition."

"It sounds like you feel guilty for saying anything," Astrid observed.

"I do. I've known him forever. We've had our ups and downs. I don't want to hurt him. But I don't want to stand by and watch him get everything. The way he always does."

Astrid was proud of Bernie. She, herself, didn't say anything mean about Karsyn. It was better not to. Those two had their own history. She could tell this was hard for Bernie, loyal as she was.

All Astrid said was, "I'm proud of you."

Back inside, the MC gathered everyone around, only to let them go again. "Due to unforeseeable circumstances we're taking a longer lunch," he announced. "Go enjoy one more hour in the sun, kids. Thanks."

There was a lot of grumbling. Everyone wanted the competition to continue.

"Do you think it's serious?" Bernie said.

"Well, yeah, maybe," Astrid said. "Hefty allegation, right?"

"But how do they even prove it?"

"Maybe they try to make him explain the inner workings here on the spot?"

"Oh, God. Maybe I shouldn't have said anything." Bernie frowned. She was still holding the clipboard.

She brought the pen up to her lips and started chewing on the end of it.

"You told the truth," Astrid said, wanting to reassure her. "There's nothing wrong with telling the truth."

"I feel like shit. Do you think he saw me? Do you think he'll trace it back to me?" Bernie started shaking.

Astrid stroked her back and told her it would be okay.

They went back inside and took their spots in the bleachers. The MC looked serious. Karsyn's team was nowhere to be found. Astrid had not noticed them leave, but their robot wasn't on the floor. Her stomach sank when she thought about what this would do to Bernie. But from where she was sitting, justice had been served.

Bernie was staring straight ahead, on the verge of tears. Astrid squeezed her arm and felt her tense up.

The MC said, "Sorry for the delay. As you may notice, we are down one robot. One of the teams was disqualified. I'd like to stress at this time that the point of this competition is not winning, but building.

I'm sure you've all learned valuable skills along the way. Skills that you can take with you into your careers, regardless of what you focus on. All right, let's get to the final battle."

The airhorn sounded. Bernie was a mess of emotions, as far as Astrid could tell. So, not a cyborg. Quite the opposite. A mushy, complicated human being. Astrid loved her for it.

Bernie's glasses fogged up while she controlled Robbie. Everyone yelled and screamed. Azi and Ranj were super loud. Louder than ever.

"Over there!"

"That one!"

"Get it!"

"You got it!"

And again they managed six boxes right before the alarm signalled the end. The feeling was like no other. Astrid's entire year of struggle vanished in that one glorious moment as the MC pronounced them the winning team of this year's battle.

♥ ♥ ♥

On the bus ride home, Astrid and Bernie sat next to each other, their legs touching the whole time. The heat of it, the electricity, combined with the biggest win Astrid had ever experienced, was such a high. She was on top of the world.

Bernie looped her arm in Astrid's. Despite Bernie's mixed feelings, she did look pleased. Astrid was happy to see it. All she wanted was for Bernie to enjoy the triumph. Enjoy the culmination of what they had accomplished together.

Astrid saw Aliyah glance over at them. Aliyah's eyes were focused right on their linked arms and the way their thighs seemed to be glued together. She raised an eyebrow and smiled. She knew exactly what was going on.

Astrid could feel herself blushing. Aliyah gave a knowing look and turned her attention out the window.

23 Pocket Girlfriend

A COUPLE OF DAYS after the competition, Astrid got a phone call.

"This is David from the head of the Mechatronics Department at UBC."

Okaaay, Astrid kept herself from saying.

"I saw you at the battle, Astrid. Congratulations on your team's win. I was just talking with Aliyah about you. She mentioned you had not committed to a post-secondary institution yet."

"That's true," Astrid said. She hadn't committed because she hadn't been accepted anywhere. But he didn't have to know that.

"Well, we'd like to offer you a one-year scholarship at UBC."

Is this some kind of prank call? Astrid wondered. "Seriously?" she asked.

"Yes."

"Okay!" Her voice chirped as she said it. It was really more of a "Hell, yes!" situation. But she didn't want to swear.

He gave her some details about coming to UBC to fill out forms. *Holy moly.*

The one person she had to tell was Bernie. She pedalled so hard to Bernie's place that she thought her legs would fall off. It was uphill the whole way, but it didn't matter. All the excitement and energy flowing through her got her to Bernie's in record speed.

"I'm in. I'm in. I can't believe it," she exclaimed.

"I can." Bernie hugged her hard. "I knew it would work out for you."

They went out for cake. This was a cake-level big deal. And then for a walk on the shore of Trout Lake.

July became August and they were together. There were still no labels. Astrid and Bernie didn't call themselves girlfriends. They weren't lovers. Astrid wasn't even sure if Bernie wanted to call herself queer. She didn't ask. She didn't want to add any pressure. All she wanted was to spend as much time with Bernie as was possible.

Bernie clearly felt the same way. She came and read at the yogourt shop, waiting for Astrid to get off work. They wandered together to the park. Astrid let go of the frustrations of retail. This day, she told a quick story about a middle-aged woman having a freak-out because they ran out of gummy worms.

"You can't make this stuff up," Astrid said.

Bernie shook her head.

They found a spot. Bernie got out a picnic blanket

and started laying out lunch. Astrid saw that the book she thought Bernie was reading was actually a planner.

"Making plans for frosh week?" Astrid asked.

"Yeah, I'll probably try to find the other robot-nerds."

Astrid nodded. Their club was irreplaceable. But they would both have to try to find new friends.

"I'm already scared to meet the robot-nerds at UBC. At least I'll have Aliyah."

"Are you going to take her course?"

"I can't," Astrid said. "It's third or fourth year."

"Yeah . . . So will you take it then?"

"I love that you think I'll still be in the program." Astrid was not so sure. She had to take it bit by bit.

"You will," Bernie said with confidence. "I know you."

Astrid had a scholarship for the first year. She could get a head start on saving for the following terms. That idea felt promising.

"Yeah, maybe." Astrid said. "But it's hard to think four years into the future. I mean, what'll happen with us? Where will we be in four years?" Astrid brushed her hand against Bernie's cheek. She couldn't conceal the sadness in her questions.

"I'm not going anywhere," Bernie said. "I mean, I am. I'll be at Waterloo. But this, what we have here, doesn't have to go anywhere." She took Astrid's hand and held it.

"I miss you already," Astrid said. She hoped she didn't sound needy.

"This is the part of the story that's supposed to feel sad," Bernie said. "In a movie there'd be images of us being far apart and depressed. But I just don't see it that way. We both get to do the cool stuff we've worked so hard to do. And it's not like we can't virtually meet all the time. You'll get sick of my face, I bet."

"You always know exactly what to say," Astrid said.

Astrid was at home when Bernie called from Waterloo.

"Let me show you my room," Bernie said. She gave Astrid a virtual tour of the entire dorm. Then, Bernie took Astrid for a stroll.

From her mattress in her parents' home in Vancouver, Astrid explored the Waterloo campus. Bernie showed her the main library and cafeteria. And the outside concourse. And every weird poster and random thing that Bernie happened to notice. There were a lot.

"Bernie?" Astrid said.

"Yeah?"

"I love you."

"I love you right back."

They stared at their screens in silence. Somehow, being thousands of kilometres apart had not defined their relationship for them. They were totally connected. Even in separate provinces.

Astrid ate dinner with Bernie in Bernie's room. With the time difference, Astrid was at the lake with a picnic lunch. But she might as well have been right next to Bernie.

"I know you're far away," Astrid said. "But we're in each other's pocket at all times." Astrid was lying on her picnic blanket looking at the screen she held in her hand. The screen that connected her to Bernie.

Bernie said, "I like having a pocket girlfriend. I can take you everywhere."

"Do you like *being* a pocket girlfriend?" Astrid asked.

"I'm finally a real cyborg!"

Astrid laughed. She missed being able to share the same space with Bernie. But for now, they both needed to be exactly where they were, doing exactly what they were doing. Winter break was coming. And there was that program designing agricultural robots in Australia. Astrid and Bernie were planning to apply to it together. Astrid's heart lifted at the thought of flying off to the other end of the world with Bernie.

Astrid might be at Trout Lake and Bernie in Waterloo. And they might not have a label for what they had. But they had figured it out. Cracked the code. And all it took was love.

ACKNOWLEDGEMENTS

All my gratitude to Kat Mototsune, my editor, who nurtured this story from its very beginnings.

The Love Code was written in COVID-19 isolation. The characters kept me company while the world around us changed rapidly and anxiety levels seemed to skyrocket. In a period of so much change, it was a joy to remember that some things never do – there will always be young people who fall in love and do everything they can to pursue their dreams and that is a great comfort.

I want to thank the tremendous people in my life: Cecilia Leong, Elaine Yong, Tony Correia, Nico Dufort, Cathleen With, Bren Robbins, Shana Myara, Billeh Nickerson, Jackie Wong, Andrea Warner, Monica Meneghetti, Amanda Hamm, Salma Saadi, Robin Bennewith, Tanya Kuhn and of course my mom.

While writing this book, I got really sick for a whole month and when I recovered I quit my job.

I say this because if you're young and you're reading this I want you to know that it's okay to make big changes. Sometimes it's a lot healthier than trying to keep things the same. After leaving a job with a stable paycheck — a move that seemed somewhat self-destructive in the middle of a pandemic — I started teaching creative writing to young people over Zoom. Reading their stories reminded me of our fundamental need to connect and share.

Thank you for picking up this book and giving it a read. And if you're interested in writing one of your own, do it! If you're thinking of getting into robotics, do it! If you're thinking of taking a chance on love, do it! The world needs it. Now more than ever.